GW

Table of Contents

Chapter 1

Normally, you hear a slow drawn-out tale of how a town decayed and lost its soul through years of hard times, but not my hometown. It happened quick—in the span of three nights, to be exact.

My friends and I would run around outside, playing hide and seek, dipping and diving through the cobblestone streets. After a long day, we would head to the center of the school field, sit under the stars, and tell stories about what we would do, where we would go, and the adventures we would take when we grew up. They seemed completely achievable, if not inevitable, at our young age. The only thing that would bring our dreams to an end would be our parents calling us in for the night.

How naïve we all were. We believed this world was nothing but sunshine and rainbows, great cheese and endless crackers. It is not.

Well, not anymore, that is. To be completely honest, I haven't seen any of my friends in years; none of them lived the life we dreamed, not even one.

We'll get to exactly when the bubble of innocence burst and when our dreams and town died, but first, let me introduce myself.

My name is George Washington, but everyone calls me GW. I was named after the wisest man in town, my father. He passed when I was very young, but all the old timers used to tell me how much they looked up to him. He was the head of police, and at an early age, had come across the great pond and helped turn my hometown from a lawless small town into the safe and fun-loving community of Tails Falls. The townsfolk even built a statue for him. It once stood in the town square, and on my way home from stargazing with friends, I would stop and tell him about how I would make him proud and keep his legacy alive by keeping every one of our friends and family, especially Mum, safe.

I failed him. I failed everyone.

Our little town housed a very small two hundred and fifty of us, mostly families that had lived here for three generations or more, with only the occasional traveler stopping through for a day or two a year. Although none of them stayed long, and I had always assumed it was because it was tough to be an outsider in such a close-knit community, I would later find out that they would be cast out for one reason or another. The last person who was able to break that barrier and stay long-term was my father, and that was some twenty years ago.

Tails Falls got its name from the large waterfall at the west edge of town. It was fed by a great pond that my father said was so wide that he'd only just made it across on a boat he'd taken months to build. The tales he told were horrifying. They had god like monsters that towered over everything, near death feline encounters, building of his escape ship and the treacherous journey across the great pond. He would always end them with something about being grateful for the town we had or about not taking it for granted. I regret not doing enough of both.

We grew up in a modest home, yet my father's craftsmanship and woodwork were unmatched. Most of the families admired it and the tale that brought him to us. Our house and our neighbors were situated on the outskirts of town to the west, behind a massive rock, which kept the wind out during the winter months.

The family next door to us was Billy-John, or BJ for short, my father's righthand man, his beautiful wife, Jolene, and their son, my childhood best friend, David. BJ had saved my father's life on the night of his arrival when his boat finally succumbed to the waves and started to break apart. The tales they told of that night and their younger days over a few wobbly pops were always too big for me and David to believe. One of our favorites was about their first meeting, the night my dad arrived. BJ had brought Jolene, his girlfriend at the time, for a campfire date on the shores of the great pond. They could see a storm brewing off in the distance and what looked to be a boat rocking across the waves. Watching it come closer they spotted the captain, my dad, frantically trying to keep the ship together. The storm was battering the ship left and right when suddenly the waves became pond monsters, lifting the boat out of the water and breaking the ship up against the waves. Jolene spotted my dad lying unconscious on a piece of wreckage and BJ didn't hesitate, he went diving in after him. If it hadn't been for their date, Jolene's keen eyes or BJ risking his life swimming out to grab my father from their clutches, he would have gone over the falls or, worse yet, been eaten. I never would have existed. Although, we never did see any pond monsters, no matter how many times we snuck up the cliffs of the falls to try and find them though.

To the east edge of town was supposed to be the no-go zone but we called it the adventure zone. David and I would venture out there to play hide and seek and build forts with our friends, but we did somewhat listen. We would never get too close to the end. It was a canyon that narrowed into a black hole in the rocks no wider than a carriage. The water from the falls would flow downhill through the town and rush down the canyon at such a pace that it always made the most devilish of noises. It would sound like that was where the real pond monsters lived, and David and I never dared to go there to find them.

The town hall, police station, and school all surrounded the schoolyard and the park that held my father's statue. It was a quiet, small town with a closeness that was both admirable and challenging for a few young scallywags like David and myself, as everyone knew everything about us.

The last three nights.

First came the blockage of the waterfall that the town was named after. It was the only source of water, and it ran dry while the town slept. The next morning, the streets were lined with confused faces and worried looks. We had seen it slow before during the hottest months of summer, but no one had ever seen it like this, especially during one of the rainiest months of the year. By mid-day, you could cut the tension with a knife, the water at the city tank was dry and most families didn't keep water reserves. Water had always been the least of everyone's concerns, there had never been a day were you couldn't turn the tap on and get fresh water. Panic was going to set in so Billy-John and a few other elders got together to head up that afternoon and see if something had lodged or damned the flow, but they never returned. Panic surely set in after that.

I would see Billy-John again a few days later, but it was certainly not a happy reunion.

The second night started extra strange, as no one was supposed to be out, but we could hear blood-curdling screams and loud rumbling that shook the house. Jolene and David had come over for dinner, as BJ hadn't returned yet, but once the rumbling started, Mother rushed David and I to the basement. We could see large shadows passing by the small window, but we couldn't make them out, as they were too big to be anyone from town.

"David, are you seeing what I'm seeing? What the hell is going on out there?"

"I can't look, man. I'm trying not to cry right now," David replied.

"It feels like the earth around us is going to come crashing through the walls, and the screams are deafening. Shouldn't we be out there, trying to help people? Like, I know they think we are young but we are teenagers now and something is terribly wrong."

He didn't reply. He just sat there with his eyes glued to the little window in the corner of the basement, shaking and occasionally breaking into tears when the screams were too close for comfort.

I wasn't sure when or if we fell asleep, but emerging with the rising sun was equally as earth-shattering and emotionally crushing as the night had been. I couldn't believe my eyes.

The town was unrecognizable. The normally packed streets were barren. with almost all the houses missing, as if they had been plucked like weeds from the ground. The police station, town hall, and school were completely flattened, the streetlights were all bent over as if they had been snapped like twigs, and my father's statue was nowhere to be seen.

We walked past the holes in the ground where the homes of people we had known all our lives had once stood, and couldn't believe our eyes. All we could muster up to say was, "Where is everyone? How is this even possible?"

Sometimes, we called out people's names, only to be silenced by our mothers' fearful voices. It was completely insane, and made zero sense. How the hell did everyone vanish? Where were the damn homes?

As we approached the school, I asked the dreaded question. "Mum, Jolene, is everyone dead?"

Both of them just stared at me, completely white, with no light in their eyes. I turned to David, and he just burst into tears again.

I couldn't contain it. I snapped. "David, get it together! You aren't two years old! Do you not see that there's no time for this? We need to do something, for fu—"

Before I could finish, my Mum's hand came across my face with such force, I hadn't thought she had it in her. I was stunned. "You need to leave him alone! You need to shut your mouth and help us look for food, water, and any survivors who may be hiding or, God forbid, injured. I need you to check the rubble while Jolene and I try and find some food. And I don't want to hear another word out of you unless you find something."

I just stared at my feet and couldn't muster up a reply. Mum very rarely scolded me, and I couldn't remember her ever hitting me. I quickly turned tail and started for the mound that used to be the police station. David sulked behind me, still weeping. I wanted to punch him, partly for being weak, but mostly for making me fear my mother for the first time in my life.

As I reached for my face to try and rub away the sting, the ground beneath me shifted, and I fell straight into the basement.

"You okay, GW? What happened?" David yelled.

"Stop yelling! I fell down a damn hole—what do you think happened? I'm fine, you idiot! Go get our mums or find some damn rope or something!" I snapped back. Instantly, I started muttering about him being the one who should have been in the damn hole.

But as soon as his silhouette disappeared, and I was left in the darkness, I could sense something watching me. My anger immediately turned to fear. "Who's there?"

No response.

"Show yourself!"

All that came back was a tiny scraping noise and what sounded like wheezing.

I started screaming for David and my mother. "*Help me! There's something down here! Get me out of here, please!*"

I turned and started trying frantically to climb out, which sent more debris coming crashing towards me, making the hole to the sky even larger. With that came more light. I whipped around in fear, thinking I was about to get mauled by something, only to see a hand and a pair of eyes under a pile or rubble only a few feet from where I landed.

"Oh, my god, are you okay? What happened here? How bad are you hurt?" I must have rhymed off a hundred questions as I clawed at the debris to free them.

The man I had thought was a monster turned out to be Rud, the town drunk. He was only a few years older than me, but had made quite a name for himself as the black sheep of the town.

"Holy shit, man, you scared the hell out of me. Are you okay?"

"I...I...don't know," he replied, obviously still inebriated from the night before.

"Can you stand? Do you know what happened here? Do you know where everyone is?"

"Last I can remember was Officer Joe throwing me in the tank for the night. I think I was pissing on the station gate. The whole place started shaking and spinning when I closed my eyes, and the next second, I wake up, and I'm stuck under all of this shit with one hell of a splitting headache." Rud slurred out his reply.

"You may be one of the luckiest drunks of all time, you know that? Everyone is gone, full homes are missing, and the station and school are flattened."

"You fucking with me, little man? GW, have you lost your mind, or have I? And am I dreaming right now?" he replied as the look in his eyes started to come back to life, the drunken fog suddenly lifting, as if he'd been slapped sober.

"No, Rud, I'm not fucking with you! The whole fucking town is gone. David, Jolene, and my mum are up top right now looking for any survivors. And who are you calling little man? You're like two years older than me."

"I need to sit do—ughh, woahhhh." Rud hurled before he could finish his sentence, though he continued intermittently trying to get words out, which I could only assume were similar to my barrage of questions as I pulled the debris off of him.

He hadn't finished wiping his mouth afterwards before we heard a thud behind us and turned to see a dangling rope. "GW, are you okay? Are you able to climb up?" Mum called down.

"I'm good, Mum, and I found Rud! The dumb drunk just puked everywhere, and it reeks!"

"What the fuck, kid!? I know I'm a little bit tipsy, but I'm not deaf or stupid!" Rud replied angrily.

"Are you serious right now, GW? Get up here now before I come down there and slap you again. Do not speak about your elders like that. I don't care how screwed up this situation is. That is no excuse," Mum shot back.

Elders? He's only a few damn years older than me, I thought before I reached for the rope. Stopping for a moment to touch my cheek, I noticed that the stinginess was gone, but the mental scar was still fresh.

We both climbed out and found not just my mum, David, and Jolene; they had been joined by Jed the farmer and his daughter Bissy. Jed's wife wasn't there, and neither was their son Joey.

Jed and David were holding jugs of water, while Bissy and Jolene were carrying burlap sacks with some food they had found. Only Mum would look me in the eye, and I knew right away that now wasn't the time to talk.

We all headed back up the hill to our house with Rud in tow, as he had to stop every few feet to gag and heave up what alcohol was left in him. I started to feel sorry for the guy, and held back to keep him moving. It was starting to get late in the day, and I certainly didn't want to be outside as the sun started to go down.

The silence continued over dinner, as none of us had eaten all day, and what we had found surely wasn't going to last us more than a day. I peered around the table over my bowl, and no one dared to look at each other, but to my damn surprise, it was David who broke the silence. "Jed, what happened to your wife? Where is Joey?" he asked.

"David, this isn't the time. Don't you see we're all eating quietly?" Jolene interrupted.

"No, no, Jolene, it's okay. These two boys are going to have to hear it eventually." As Jed started to explain, Bissy burst into tears and ran out of the kitchen. "My Delores and Joey were outside pulling the laundry down off the line when the shaking started. When I heard Delores scream, I ran for the door, only to see a giant shadow engulf her and Joey, pulling them kicking and screaming into the sky. I couldn't believe what I saw, but as I went to rush out the door after them, Bissy grabbed my arm. Both of them vanished so fast, straight up into the sky! Before I could even compute what was happening, the house started to shake and crack, sending Bissy and I scrambling for the cold cellar at the back of the house. As we closed the doors, we could see the darkness come crashing through the ceiling, and the whole house was lifted into the dark sky. My Delores, Joey, and the whole fucking house within seconds—all sucked up into the sky." Jed broke into tears and couldn't stop repeating, "My Delores, my son."

All of us were stunned, mouths wide open, just staring at Jed. He was the hard farmer who you never wanted to mess with, and here he was, completely broken. None of it made any sense either—darkness lifting houses into the sky and grabbing people!?

"This is madness. I can't believe this. Do you have any alcohol, Jolene!?" Rud spoke up for the first time since telling me to shut up back in the hole.

"I was going to save it for after we put the kids down, but why not? Sounds like all of us need it. I'll be back in a second. The bottle is going to be really dusty, but I'm sure the liquor will still do the job," Mum replied, then walked over to Dad's old desk, opened the bottom drawer, and pulled out a very old bottle that had been given to him at his retirement dinner.

Rud looked at me and patted me on my back. "GW, go grab some glasses, will ya?"

I went to the cupboard, grabbed stacked three glasses per hand, and slinked back to the table, hoping no one would notice the extra two for David and I. Mum saw it right away.

"Put four down here." She filled them to the absolute brim and slid them across the table to Rud, Jed, Jolene, and herself. "Now, put those other two down," she said with a smile and poured out two half glasses for me and David.

"Addy, David is too young," Jolene replied with a tiny smirk. I couldn't believe she used the name Addy. My mother's name was Adeline, and the last time I heard anyone refer to my mum as Addy, it had been my father.

"Jol, they are sixteen and after today, I think whatever innocence they still had took a big hit, and at the worst, it will help them sleep," Mum replied.

Grabbing my glass, I took a big whiff of my glass, and instantly felt the burn in my nostrils. It smelt like father's bedtime stories. I started to tear up, but didn't have time to let them fall, as everyone reached out their glasses to cheers.

"Cheers to my husband GW Sr., to BJ, to Delores and Joey, to everyone of Tails falls, and last, to all of you," Mum recited, finishing with a big group clink of glasses.

We all took a big swig and burst out laughing as David instantly spat it all out over the table.

"Guess his innocence wasn't ready to be given up," Rud blurted out to even more laughter.

As the adults kept filling their glasses, laughing and crying, I slowly replaced my empty glass with the other half-full one David had left with no one noticing. The sensation and nostalgia of drinking my father's favorite drink was overwhelming.

Soon, the rest of them were howling at my belligerent nonsensical rants about nothing, and I was easily found out for drinking David's leftovers. Even Mum took a few shots at my slurring before quickly putting an end to it when I started to talk about how beautiful Bissy was. "Alright, alright, wee little boy. I think you have had enough. It's time you join your lover girl and buddy downstairs for bed!" she quipped.

I protested and proclaimed I was a man, to everyone's delight, as it came out completely wrong—"Wee wee, little boy? Me man." Or something like that.

Rud was in hysterics and came back at me with, "Me man with little wee wee."

Mum took me downstairs and set me up beside David, who was long asleep, then gave me a kiss goodnight. It almost felt like a regular night, except for the fact that the world was spinning like a record.

Before I knew it though, my blissful night turned again into horror when I was shaken awake by David. "Get up man, get your clothes on! The shaking is back!" he yelled.

"Fuck, what's going on? I don't feel so good, why is the world spinning?" I replied, still drunk from my two half-glasses.

"The shaking is back; the adults are all rushing around, getting the food and water packed. We need to get ready to leave *now*!" Bissy responded as David rummaged through his pack.

I could feel the thuds through the ground now, and the light was flickering in the rafters. Reality set in, and the memories of the day before shot back into focus. My clothes were just out of reach, and even under the stress of waking up to the craziness, I was embarrassed to have Bissy see me in my underwear. She was like a sister to me and growing up she had seen me in my skids countless times but that was when we were kids.

As if she'd read my mind, she walked over, grabbed my clothes, and threw them at me. "Let's go, GW! I saw Addy put you to bed, so I've already seen you in your underwear!"

I was pretty sure I went a stark shade of red until another giant thud sent a few small rocks tumbling between us as they broke away from the foundation. That was enough to light the fire under my ass I needed, and sent my ego right out the window.

The three of us grabbed what we could and ran up the stairs. Before we could reach the top of the stairs, the door flung open, and everyone started yelling to get back down the stairs. Everyone was clambering over each other, and I could see the house coming down behind them.

"The window! Push open the window! We have to climb out and run for it. Leave everything!" Jed screamed.

"Mum, did you get Dad's lucky baseball cap!?" I asked, frantically running over to her as Rud and Jed started to kick out the window.

"No, there was no time, GW!" she replied without looking up at me.

I didn't even hesitate and continued right past her and straight up the stairs. Before she could even say anything, I was scurrying under the rubble in front of the door. His lucky white hat with the black brim always hung on the wall behind his desk, he always put it on when he got home from work and promised it to me one day. "When your head and life experiences get big enough, it will be yours," he always used to say.

Crawling along of the floor under collapsed beams and over shattered family photos from the house you grew up in is terrifying. If I had thought for a millisecond, I never would have gone, and with each movement of the shadows through the debris, the fear started to set in. There was no turning back now, though; nothing could take my last physical memory of my father from me.

After what felt like an hour, I had finally reached my father's desk, which was lying half-crushed under the beam he'd described as the belly of his ship. My heart sank. The wall that the hat had hung on for years was gone, and the hat was nowhere in sight.

At that moment, everything went dark, and I froze. I was exposed, out in the open, and Jed's story of Joey and his wife's demise flashed through my mind as I looked up to see a monstrous black figure outlined by the moon behind it. It was taller than anything I had ever seen. Even the waterfall paled in comparison.

As what looked to be one of its arms moved down towards me, the moonlight beamed over its shoulder onto the rubble directly in front of the monster, and my eyes no longer fixated on the monster, but the bright white fabric now encased in moonlight. It was the hat! It was right there, right in front of the beast.

My legs lunged forward before I could even think about it. I grabbed the hat and dove back under the desk, squeezing through the rubble and weaving my way back towards the basement. As I feverishly crawled, the rubble around me was flung left and right as the shadow tried to find me.

With no time to breathe and no time to scream, I made it to the stairs and threw myself down them. Jed and Rud were helping Bissy out the window when I came crashing down. Everyone was out but Jed, Rud, and my mother. "Go, go, go! It's right behind me!" Grabbing my mother's hand, I pulled her close and lifted her up out the window.

"You got balls, kid," Rud said as he grabbed me by the back of my neck and the belt of my pants and heaved me out the window behind Mum.

Rud came next, and as he reached back in for Jed, the shadow came crashing through the floor, crushing Jed in an instant. One second, he was staring at me, and the next, he was gone. All I could see was his broken and lifeless arm hanging from the rubble. It happened so damn fast.

Bissy tried to run for her father, but Rud grabbed her arm and, in one motion, threw her over his shoulder.

"Run!" he yelled as he bolted past us with Bissy bouncing violently and screaming for her father.

We all took off after Rud, trying to keep up. He'd boasted about his high school track days the night before, when we were all drinking, and he hadn't been lying. I would have never believed the town drunk could run this fast, but here he was, with a flailing girl on his back, pulling away from us with every stride.

I headed straight for the canyon, legs pumping below me so fast that I didn't dare turn around. Once we hit the footpath that tracked along the dried-up riverbed, we dipped into the darkness of some overhanging rocks to catch our breath. The tremors had stopped, and it was pitch-black in the canyon, as the moon had slipped behind the ridge on the north side.

Bissy had stopped screaming, but after Rud put her down, she curled up and rocked back and forth, shaking profusely. I knew there was nothing I could say, so I walked over, took my jacket off, and placed it around her. Rud was gassed, and Jolene and my mum were heaving against the back wall, trying to breathe.

That was when I noticed I couldn't see David. The last time I could remember seeing him was when we passed the school.

"David?" Jolene said between gasps.

"Last I saw him was as we were passing the school. He was right on my tail," I replied.

She looked at my Mum and Rud, and they both just shook their heads.

Jolene instantly started screaming his name, and Mum was quick to grab her and put her hand over her mouth. "Shhh, Jolene! I'm sure he's fine, we can try and go back..." Mum whispered before screeching in pain as Jolene bit her hand, then went running out of the cave. She went left, back down the dark trail, yelling for David at the top of her lungs.

"What's she doing? Stop yelling, dammit," Rud muttered.

Right before Jolene was out of sight, a giant light beamed down from the sky, almost as if the moon had concentrated all of its light right on her. Just as Jed had described the night prior, a giant shadow engulfed her and pulled her off into the sky, screaming. As quickly as the light had appeared, it disappeared, and the screaming stopped.

Just like that, Jolene was gone.

Bissy broke the silence after a few short minutes that felt like an hour. "I can't do this! I can't go any further! My dad is gone, Joey is gone, my mother is gone, David is gone, and now Jolene is gone. For fuck's sake, the whole town is gone. We're all going to die out here!"

"We have to try and make it to the end of the canyon. If we stay here, we'll certainly die. It must know we're here now, and you saw the size of the hand that crushed your house. It could reach in here at any moment. There's no way it can follow us into the cave at the end of the canyon, though. We should be safe if we can get there," Rud replied.

"Can you still carry Bissy? I don't think she's in any headspace to run," Mum asked Rud.

He nodded and started towards Bissy, who was still shaking in the corner. Cutting him off, I said, "Give me a second to talk to her. We don't need her screaming and hitting you, as we all know the path gets rougher the closer we get to the end, and any noise will surely get us caught, like Jolene."

He nodded in approval.

"Bissy, we need to go—"

She interrupted me and again said, "I can't! Everyone is gone!"

"We need to try, not only for ourselves, but for everyone. Someone needs to live on and remember them. If we don't, then the memory of everyone, including ourselves, will be gone forever."

She looked up at me and didn't reply. She just reached out her hand, and I didn't hesitate to take it.

Rud bent down and Bissy climbed on his back, piggyback-style. "Well, this will make running a lot easier than having you over a shoulder," Rud lightheartedly said as he started for the path. "You other two ready? We can't stop again."

"We're as ready as we can be, but GW should lead," Mum replied, then looked at me and said, "GW, you will need to go in front. You know the path better than any of us, and you will need to guide us. Do not look back, and do not stop. No matter what happens, do not look back. I love you, and know you will guide us through this."

"She's right, you know. I haven't walked this path since I was a young boy, and I've had way too many brain-cell-killing drinks to remember which turns to take," Rud added.

"It's decided. GW, we need you to get us through this, and I know you can do it. You are your father's son, after all," Mum said with a kiss, knowing that last bit would light a fire under me. It worked.

"Alright, before we go—stay close, and if anything happens and we get split up, remember not to take any right turn when you come to a fork. Always go straight or left, and it will lead you to the cave," I said with my newfound leader's voice. "Remember, always straight or left, and keep quiet."

A quick pan of the ridges for any movement came back with nothing, so we started off down the trail. The hair on the back of my neck was standing up, and my heart was pounding in my chest so hard that I could swear I heard it echoing off the canyon walls. The first few moments were easy and fast-paced, as the trail slowly wound down towards the once-rushing river. Rud had lost a step from the frantic chase through town, but Mum was right on my heels.

As we were approaching the first fork, I wheeled around to give the signal to go straight, but as I turned back around, I looked up and couldn't believe my eyes. The moon was so bright, and was no longer hiding behind the ridge. It was frantically moving around the sky, beaming a ray of light down as if it were scanning the canyon for something, and that something could only be us. I could faintly see what looked to be the shadow monster controlling it.

"What the fuck is this thing? It can control the damn moon?" I muttered to myself.

Even though the fastest route was to continue going straight, we would have to pass through an exposed portion of trail and would more than likely be caught in the scanning moonlight. I dipped in between two rocks on the side of the trail to the left. Mum had seen me, but we waited to make sure Rud had too. He hadn't. Bissy and Rud were softly talking to each other, and hadn't noticed the last second change, nor the moon moving through the sky. I reached for Rud's arm to pull them in, but I missed and grabbed Bissy's leg, which brought out a massive squeal of fear from her. It was the worst-case scenario, as I had been hoping to pull them in silently so we could make our way down the trail to the left quietly.

The moon instantly beamed down on them and started growing larger, quickly engulfing all four of us in its light. The cliffs around us started to crumble, and it looked like the giant shadow monster was standing above the canyon with its legs on either side. We were blinded by the light, and were trying to break out of its borders into the darkness as we ran down the left trail towards the riverbed.

Seeing the trail lit up only a few feet in front of us at all times made jumping over the fallen tree limbs and not stumbling on exposed roots extra challenging— they only came into focus right as they were about catch our feet or hit us in the head.

David and I used to play tag on this portion of trail, as it had so many obstacles, so it was mainly muscle memory for me, and I could see why the others wanted me in the front of the pack. As we reached the riverbank, the light was starting to fall behind, and we were able to lose it as we jumped down into the muddy riverbed. The moonlight went right down the trail ahead instead of following us into the riverbed, as we had pulled away just enough for it to miss our descent.

"What the heck is this thing? It has to be huge if it can straddle the canyon and control the fucking moon," Rud exclaimed.

"I don't know, but it's going to take us forever to get to the end of the canyon through this mud, unless we risk going back up to the trail, hoping it doesn't back-track looking for us, which it will most likely do very soon, if it hasn't already," I replied.

"How far is it? I have mud up to my knees, and carrying Bissy is going to make it impossible for me to run in here," Rud shot back.

"I've never walked the riverbed before, but we're about five minutes away on the trail. The riverbed snakes, where the trail is a straight shot so maybe an extra ten or fifteen minutes, but if the mud is this deep the whole way, who knows?" I replied.

Standing almost waist-deep, Mum made the decision for us. "We should head back up to the trail and risk it. I don't think I can make it through this mud, nor do I think Rud will be able to with Bissy on his back. Even if she walked on her own, the mud would be up to her waist."

We didn't need to discuss any further after that, so we started to climb back out to the trail. The rocks were extremely slippery with my feet covered in mud, but luckily, there were plenty of roots to grab on to. I went up first and helped Mum and Bissy out. While Rud started his climb, I moved slightly up the trail, searching the sky and looking down the trail for any sign of the moon or the monster controlling it.

The coast seemed clear.

As we shook off as much mud as we could, we decided that we would walk slowly and quietly. We were getting dangerously close to sunup, and we had nowhere to hide, so if it came to it, we needed to have energy left if we needed to make another break for it.

After talking with Rud before the last chase, Bissy had started to come back out of her shellshocked state, and decided to walk so Rud could get some relief. "It will be good to get some blood moving in your legs, but stay close to me, Bissy. If anything happens, I'll pick you up, and we'll run," I heard Rud say to her.

Passing through the last bit of trail was eerily quiet and pitch-dark, with no scanning moon light, no shaking ground, and no crumbling rocks. Something felt off, but I kept reassuring myself that it was just the adrenaline wearing off. The thing that got me the most, though, was that there were no stars in the sky or wind in the canyon. It was always windy down here, and we should be able to hear the noises howling from the cave being this close. Was it because the water wasn't rushing down the river? Was the cave at the end closed off?

As we came around the last cliff and into sight of the cave, it looked to still be open, but it had grown in size, with rocks piled up on either side of the entry.

"That's it. Let's make a run for it!" Rud exclaimed.

"Something doesn't feel right, Rud. The ground is littered with jagged rocks that I don't remember being here and do you see all the rocks piled up on either side? The entry is also a lot larger." I replied.

Bissy was climbing onto Rud's back for the final sprint, and Mum was kneeling over, tying her shoes, when suddenly, the moon appeared behind us—with another in front of us at the same time. It made no sense. We were surrounded by light, and had no choice but to rush for the entrance of the cave.

I grabbed Mum by the arm and pulled her up and over the first group of jagged rocks, as she was slow on the draw. Stumbling forward, she lost one of her shoes and tripped over a sharp rock, sending us both tumbling. We watched as Rud and Bissy made it past the light in front of us and disappeared into the cave.

Before I could get Mum back to her feet, we were engulfed by the shadow of what looked like a massive hand. It grasped us both and began to lift us up towards the moon. It was devoid of any fur, and I could feel the pulse of its heartbeat through its skin as it held us tightly.

Instinct kicked in, and I chomped down on the hand, puncturing the skin, which caused a rumbling groan from the monster. Before I could get my teeth loose from its flesh, the grip loosened, and I watched in horror as Mum slipped out of its grasp and plummeted towards the rocky ground below. I didn't see the impact, as the monster regained its grip on me, but I knew it in my bones and in my heart.

I had just killed my mother.

Chapter 2

Curled up, slowly coming to from what felt like the deepest sleep I'd ever had, I wanted to believe it was just a nightmare, and didn't want to open my eyes to find out if it wasn't. I kept imagining I was at home, curled up in my bed, hoping my mother was going to come in and tell me to stop being lazy. The tears started to come, making it impossible to keep my eyes closed any longer.

Surrounded by what smelled like woodchips, I could hear two people talking. They sounded like Rud and Bissy. Maybe it was just a bad dream.

Pushing my way out of the warm darkness, I was met with a blinding light and two silhouettes staring off into what looked like a white abyss. *Am I dead? Is this heaven?* I thought. *If it is, why are they here, and where is Mum?*

Rud's voice interrupted my thoughts of doom. "GW, you okay, man? You slept a long time."

Bissy lunged at me and wrapped her arms around me, sobbing. "I am so sorry, GW. I am so, so sorry about your Mum."

Her words and embrace crushed me. My legs went limp, and she followed me to the ground to continue holding me.

How were they here? How was I with them? The last I had seen them, they were running through the entrance of the cave.

I had so many questions, but I couldn't get a word out in between the tears.

"Take your time, man. Let it out," Rud said as he dropped down beside us and put a hand on my back.

"You were asleep for a whole day, GW. I was starting to think you weren't going to wake up," Bissy said softly.

As if he knew all the questions I was thinking, Rud started to explain what had happened. "As soon as we reached the cave, a gate dropped down behind us, and we were trapped. The rocks piled up had concealed a cage that was behind the rocks, but in front of the actual cave. They knew where we were going, it was almost as if they were herding us. After you bit that one, and your mother—well, you know—they stuck you with something, and you went completely limp. We thought they had killed you. Then, they put you into the cage with us, and we could feel your heart beating."

"Where are we now?"

"Stand up, come over here, and I'll show you. You won't believe your eyes," Rud said, extending his hand to help me up.

We were in a glass box with giant wood shavings on the ground. There was a massive bottle with what looked to be water hanging upside down on one of the walls, and a brown house was standing in the middle. The top of the glass prison had what looked to be a screen covering it to keep us from climbing out.

As I walked to the front with Rud and Bissy, I realized they were right: I didn't believe my eyes. There were glass prisons just like our own lining the walls around us in a giant white room. We were at the very top of what looked to be a massive shelving unit, so I couldn't see the ones below us, but by counting the rows on the other side, there must have been over a hundred prisons just like our own. If there were three rats in each, that would mean the whole town could be here.

"Who have you seen? Is everyone here? Is David here? What about Jolene? Bissy, are your brother and mother here? What the *fuck* is this place?" I asked frantically.

"You won't believe this, but BJ is in the prison next to us, and, so far, we have been able to identify almost half of the town. We're hoping Joey and Bissy's mother are in one of the cages below us. Jolene is over there, third row down from the top and two rows in from the left. No sign of David yet," Rud replied.

"BJ is alive!?" I exclaimed.

"Yes. He was asking about you and David. I talked to him last night, but I warn you, he's not doing so well after hearing about David's disappearance," Rud replied.

"I need to talk to him as soon as possible, but first, can you tell me anything more about where we are?"

"All I know is what you see, and that the shadow monsters aren't actually shadows. They're giant animals that BJ called humans. He said your father had told him all about them after his journey from across the pond. They're really odd-looking, as they only have fur on their heads, and they seem to want us alive, as they've been dropping in food and refilling those giant water bottles every few hours," Rud answered.

"Father told me stories about two legged giants but I always thought it was him trying to scare me. Is BJ awake?" I replied.

"Go knock on the glass over there and see," Rud said.

I paused for a moment. How was I going to look him in the eye? I had no idea what I would say to him, as he always used to tell me to look after David when we were out playing. Since I was a few months older and a bit harder in spirit, he'd always looked to me as sort of guiding figure for his son. He was definitely misguided for thinking that, as I was certainly the reason David would get in trouble ninety-nine percent of the time, but I always told him I would.

Just like my promises to father, I know I failed him.

Swallowing my guilt, I reached out and pounded on the glass. It didn't take long before I saw him—my father's right-hand man. Rud was right; he looked like shit. Walking over, I could see him wiping the wet fur under his eyes, trying to make it look like he was just waking up.

"I am so sorry—" I started before he raised a hand to stop me.

"No, GW. Do not even start with that shit. I know David is below us somewhere in one of these godforsaken glass boxes from hell. I'm the one who is sorry. Adeline—your mother, I mean—was a beautiful soul, and we all knew how proud she was to have you as her son. You kept her going after your father passed," BJ said as his voice started to quiver. He continued with, "How are you holding up?"

I broke again, tears streaming down my fur and my uncontrollable breathing started to fog up the glass. "I killed her, BJ. If I hadn't bit that monster, she would be here right beside me, talking to you right now. It's all my fault. If only I—"

He slammed a hand against the glass to interrupt me. "There you go again, you shut your damn mouth right there, you hear me!" he yelled. He didn't stop at that. "Do you know what your father used to say to me? 'If life bites you, you fucking bite it back!' Your father would have done the same damn thing in your position. All of us would have! If I hear you say you killed her ever again, I'll break through this glass and give you a right lashing."

I had experienced a BJ lashing many times before after father passed, and the fear of it almost instantly turned my eye faucets off. It didn't stop the guilt or the self-loathing, but it did help me regain some composure.

"Listen, GW: your father told me about these… what you called 'monsters.' They were what your father was running from when he came across the pond all those years ago. He called them humans, and explained how they ruled the world outside of Tails Falls. At first, I didn't believe him, until one day he took me to see them. It scared the living shit out of me to see beings so damn big compared to us. Walking damn furless giants. Why do you think he was the only outsider ever to last more than a day or two in town? As soon as they would start talking about the outside world, scaring the townsfolk, we kicked them out. We hoped the day would never come where our worlds would intersect, but we were naïve to think they wouldn't. We tried to plan escape routes or contingency plans, but after your dad passed, I got complacent. We were just so damn sheltered, and life was good. If anyone is to blame for your mother—or for anyone, for that matter—it should be me," BJ explained.

Then, his eyes darted to the middle of the room. "One of them is back," he said. "Look, this is one of the men. There's a woman who comes, drops food in, and refills the water. She should be arriving soon. We're still not sure what they want from us or why they have us in these glass prisons."

"Has anyone been able to talk to them?"

"No. They can't understand us, from what I can tell. We can certainly understand them, though. This piece of enormous shit called me cute. Can you believe that?" BJ replied with a smirk.

He'd always had a sense of humor, so it was good to see he still had some left in the tank after the past few days of being locked up in such a terrifying place, wondering about his family.

We moved to the front of the glass so we could get a better vantage point for watching the human who had entered the room. It was horrifically tall; I would say over a hundred rats tall, as I didn't have anything from memory that I could compare its enormity to. It was truly something to behold. I could see why my father and BJ tried to keep them a secret from everyone. It was absolutely earth-shattering to realize how small I really was.

It wasn't that we all believed we were the top of the food chain or anything. We had seen and heard many stories about all different types of dogs that roamed the plains past the forests above the falls where the four-legged felines stalked the ground and the pigeons and birds patroled the sky. We also would see the odd slimy frog around the edges of the great pond and every so often a fish head or skeleton would come over the falls. Those would make you think twice about going for a swim north of the falls, but humans were on a whole different level of freakiness. They were what some might call God-sized.

This human was muttering to itself, and I couldn't make out what it was saying through the glass, but it seemed happy, almost joyous. It started to move very oddly, almost as if it were dancing.

"Is it singing?"

"Who knows, GW? Who knows? But if that's dancing, it should really come to a Rat-dig and take a few lessons," BJ chuckled.

Our joking ended very abruptly, as the human reached into the prison beside Jolene's and grabbed what looked to be Goe the baker. It brought him over to the table and laid him out as Goe screamed and flailed. Pinning him down with one of its gargantuan hands, still muttering and dancing oddly, it opened a drawer and grabbed what looked to be a giant measuring tape. It looked just like the one mum had used to use to measure my height each season change. It stretched the tape out from tail to snout, and then wrapped it around Goe's body and pulled it so tight I thought his eyes were going to pop out.

"The worst part is next," BJ said, interrupting my horror. "You may want to look away."

The human went back to the drawer, grabbed some odd-shaped device, and put Goe's ear in it. There was a crunching sound, followed by Goe's shrieks.

I almost looked away, but curiosity got the better of me. It was almost like the earrings some of the old timers had, but with a big number on it.

"They're measuring us and tagging us. He's the twentieth one I've seen, and it has been making its way down each row. At this rate, it will be Jolene's turn later today, and I don't know if I'll be able to take it," BJ said with a frog in his throat.

After the human was done tagging Goe, he took him, put him back, and grabbed his next victim. I couldn't stomach watching another one. *How did BJ sit through twenty of these already?* I wondered.

"I don't think I can watch this again, BJ. If you need me, I'll be hiding in the shack. How long do you think we have 'til it makes its way over to our side?"

"If it goes at the rate they have been going, tomorrow, probably around midday. We'll have to see which direction they start with, but hopefully, I can catch a glimpse of David, so I'll be watching the whole day," BJ replied.

"Do you want me to come back shortly so I can be with you when Jolene goes up?"

"I'll be fine, lil' man. You just go worry about Bissy, and make sure Rud's okay. His alcohol withdrawal will be kicking in soon, and it's never pretty. Be careful, and make sure you keep your patience with him. He can get really mouthy," BJ replied, right on character in his worrying-about-others way.

Walking away from BJ, my guilt fading, I couldn't help but think about how strong he really was and why my father had formed such a lasting brotherly bond with the man. He really was like a second father to me and so many others in the town. If he hadn't been around all the time, I can only imagine what pain I would have caused for my mother.

Luckily, before I could think too much about my mother, Rud came out of the shack, sweating like crazy. "You alright, Rud? You look like how I feel after seeing what they just did to Goe the baker!"

"Man, I'm getting the shakes pretty bad, and it's hot as all hell in that shack. You saw the tagging, didn't you? I can't watch that shit, especially fucking sober," he replied before going over to the water bottle and letting it drain onto his head.

"How is Bissy doing?"

"I don't fucking know, man. Just let me sulk out here. I'm no fun to be around right now," he shot back at me.

Yup, BJ was right. The withdrawals are kicking in, I thought.

I didn't even bother replying; I just turned and ducked into the shack. Bissy was asleep on a makeshift bed in the back-right corner as I entered, so I made one for myself on the corner across from her, leaving space for Rud to make one by the door for easy access to fresh air.

There was no way I was going to sleep after being knocked out for a whole day, but at least I could sit down, gather myself, and try to make sense of what was going on around me.

No sense was to be found sitting there, though, I'll tell you that much. I couldn't move past the size of the human I had just seen and what it did to Goe. Knowing that tomorrow, I would have to experience firsthand what I had just watched, it didn't take long before the fear started to kick in. I started to feel sick and began to sweat, as if I were going through the same withdrawals Rud was going through. As I got up to try and go for some fresh air, the shack started to spin, and I stumbled out the door and hurled the moment I got outside. "Get it together," I tried to tell myself, but it didn't help. The taste of my salty sweat was soothing and unsettling all at the same time.

Rud took a break from drowning himself to come help me sit under the water bottle, which he'd jimmy-rigged open. We didn't say anything to each other for a good ten minutes, but just sat there soaking in our own pains and sorrows before Rud started to apologize. "Sorry for snapping at you back there, kid. Well, I guess you aren't a kid anymore, so sorry for that, too. Got a lot of respect for you, lil' man."

"It's okay, Rud. You do realize that I'm only a few years younger than you, too, right?" I replied.

"No, it really isn't. I've been drunk every day for the past five years since my mother and father died. The last few days has been the most I've interacted with anyone other than a bottle or with BJ putting me in the drunk tank," Rud explained, completely bypassing the age comment.

"I never knew anything more than my mother saying you were a good guy, but fell into some hard times. Like, I had heard the stories but didn't put much weight into them as I know after my father died, I rebelled pretty hard, but having BJ next door to help set me straight definitely quelled the anger pretty quickly. I'm really sorry to hear about your mother and father. I never knew them."

"Yeah. For as much shit as I caused in town, BJ was always there for me, too. Well, at least as a good shoulder for me to drunkenly cry on, but, being older and living on my own, I never took his help seriously enough, as by the time I woke up the next day, all I could think about was drinking the pain away again," Rud said with tears in his eyes.

"I can tell you, even without knowing your parents, they would have been extremely proud of how you helped save Bissy. You could have outrun us and left us all, but you didn't. Your first thoughts were to grab the slowest one of us and lead the way. You're good shit, Rud. I'm grateful I fell down that hole and found you."

"I'm grateful you did too, man," he replied, embracing me in a hug.

We both needed that hug, although the good feelings only lasted maybe a second, if that. After we got up and shook ourselves off, we saw BJ, his face smashed up against the glass, slamming his fists against the invisible barrier that held us captive.

It was Jolene's turn.

We ran over to be with him. As we got there, we saw her look at him, reach an arm out to him and mouth, "I love you." It was heart-breaking, like a giant gut punch, and, again, the feeling of wanting to vomit returned as a tag was punched into her ear.

"I love you, Jolene! I'm sorry! I'm so very sorry," BJ repeated over and over again as he pounded the glass. His hands were going blue, and if the human had put Jolene back any later than he did, I swear, he would have broken both of his hands on that glass.

"You alright, BJ? Your hands are blue, man," Rud asked.

BJ didn't respond, but turned his back and walked straight into his shack. It dawned on me then that I hadn't seen any other rats in BJ's cage. Was he alone over there, crying uncontrollably? I knew he was a strong man, but no one should be going through this alone.

Rud and I didn't say a word to each other after BJ left. We just walked back to our shack and laid down on our makeshift beds. I assume Rud was contemplating the madness we just watched, just as I was. For me, watching a man you looked up to your entire life and saw as being unbreakable completely lose it was eye-opening.

But everyone had their breaking point. No one was unbreakable, and certainly not me.

I was slowly drifting to sleep after what felt like an eternity of staring at the ceiling when suddenly, it lifted off the walls, revealing the eyes of a human. The whole place was shaking, as it had the entire glass prison in its hands.

As I put my feet down off the mound of woodchips I had piled up to sleep on, they splashed right into ankle-deep water. Rud fell off his bed to a panicked splash, and Bissy was stiff as a board, just staring out the open ceiling.

"Rud! We left the water bottle jammed. The whole prison is flooded!" I squealed.

Rud didn't have a chance to speak before a gentle female voice came out of the giant human's mouth. "What happened here, lil' ones? How did you flood your home? This just won't do. I won't have you little rascals drowning, now. Let's get this cleaned up," the female human said to us reassuringly.

I tried to yell at her to let us go, but her reply made me realize she couldn't understand me as I had her. "Don't squeal, lil' one. Momma Jenny will get this cleaned up quickly and get you fresh bedding."

I tried again, this time with a lot more profanity, but she didn't even look at me this time. BJ was right—they couldn't understand us.

"Her name is Jenny!? And she fucking thinks she's our momma!? Are these things mad!?" I said angrily to myself.

She gently grabbed each of us and put us on the table. Instantly, we all tried to run for it until we reached the edge and saw how high up we were. It would be certain death if we jumped.

"Don't you guys try it. Here, wait in here," Jenny said as she placed a giant box over us. It was pitch-black. We huddled together, shivering in fear. We could hear her out there banging away on the glass, murmuring about cleaning this and filling that. After what felt like hours, she lifted the box off and proceeded to tell us how cute we were for cuddling each other.

"'Cuddling each other?' We're fucking scared to death," I replied, not expecting a reply from so-called Momma Jenny!

She scooped us up and plopped us back into our prison, which had been freshly stocked with wood-chips and a bigger shack. She then proceeded to plop our whole prison—or what she called a home—back on the shelf.

We all scurried back into the shack, absolutely shell-shocked, as she left the room and turned off the lights.

Not a single rat was stirring that night, and it took us a good hour or two before we started to remake our beds. Bissy still hadn't said a word, and Rud had kept it to small talk about the new sleeping arrangements. We had decided to make one big bed in the center of the shack, and that was about it. Neither Rud or I slept, and we weren't sure if Bissy had fallen asleep, as you couldn't even hear or see her breathing, she was so still.

In the morning, when the lights came on, we peeked outside to find some carrots and leafy greens sitting on our doorstep. Rud and I quickly grabbed it and dragged it in.

The three of us were sitting there munching silently when we heard the first scream. The last of the measuring and tagging had begun already.

It was impossible to stomach eating any more food at that point, so I decided to go and see if BJ was out and if I could catch a glimpse of David, Joey, or Bissy's mother.

BJ wasn't there, so I sat and watched as, one-by-one, our neighbors below us were dragged out, measured, and tagged. Almost the whole town was here, trapped in this hell with us. Each time it came to the tagging part, I had to look away.

Then, right as Rud came to sit with me, the humans reached the row directly below us, and out came Joey, and then Bissy's mother. I didn't dare call for Bissy—I couldn't have her see this—but at least we knew they were alive.

"Rud, when they put Bissy's mother back, go tell her they're alive. It will be our turn soon, so try and bury her in the bed."

"I don't think that will work, GW. They know how many of us are in here," he replied.

"Just do it. This is a different human from yesterday, and that crazy Momma Jenny lady isn't here. BJ looked to be alone, so maybe there aren't exactly three of us in each prison," I shot back.

Rud ran off immediately when he saw the man going for the prison two places over from us. It was worth a try. If I could save Bissy from having to be manhandled and tagged, at least I would have done something worth a damn in my life.

I went over to knock for BJ as they reached the cell beside us, which had a few rats I had never seen before in it. I wanted to see if he'd seen David, but he didn't answer.

Returning to the shack, I found Rud finishing up burying Bissy. "We're next. Here is the plan: We sit on the bed and don't move when it pulls the shack away.

When it puts us both back, we immediately go back to sitting on the bed. If it tries to move us, bite it. It's our only chance to keep Bissy safe," I told Rud.

He nodded, and we jumped up and sat there silently until the inevitable moment came. We heard the screen come off, and our shack was pulled back. The hand that came in after us had a bite mark exactly where I had bit when it held Mum and I. Rage filled me immediately, and instinct got the better of me again. I lunged to try and bite it again.

The giant hand retreated momentarily, and the man looked at me and said, "Oh, oh, look who it is. I remember you, you little bastard. I hate doing this, but I'm going to enjoy this one."

He grabbed me by the tail and hung me upside down, dangling over the ground. I couldn't do anything as he carried me over to the table and slammed me down, pinning my arms back with only two fingers. It felt like my bones were going to explode under his weight. He wrapped the tape around my stomach and pulled it so tight I could feel my eyes push towards the edges of their sockets. The pain was excruciating, and I blacked out momentarily from lack of oxygen.

Then, grabbing the tagging device, he looked at me and smiled. "You get two for biting me," he said as he punched a tag into each ear. I was so mad and in so much pain I couldn't even scream.

He didn't release my arms until he had my tail in his other hand. Luckily, my arms still worked, and as he brought me close to his face and started to say something, I realized he was close enough that I could reach the tip of his nose. I swung as hard as I could and scratched him across his fat, furless snout.

"You motherfucker!" he screamed.

"Bob! You okay?" Momma Jenny said as she burst into the room behind us.

"I'm fine, but this feisty little shit was the one that bit me the other night, and now, he just scratched the shit out of my nose," the man replied as he wiped a drop of blood away.

"Ha-ha. He clearly does not like you. But can you blame him?" she replied with a chuckle.

The man just grunted and threw me against the back of the glass prison, knocking me out cold.

I woke up a few hours later. I was lying on the bed in the middle of our shack with Rud and Bissy standing over me. My vision was blurry, but a smile instantly came to my face as I realized Rud had a tag, but Bissy didn't.

"It worked, man. It fucking worked, but goddamn, you pissed him off. As he was doing me, the blood started to drip faster, and he quickly tagged me, put me back, and ran out of the room, swearing like a madman," Rud explained, chuckling. "He came back a few minutes later with a bandage over his nose and then moved over to BJ's cell."

"Is BJ alright?" I inquired.

"Oh, yeah, dude. Jolene was a mess but BJ saw what you did and went through the whole thing with a damn smile on his face. He just smiled at Jolene and blew her a kiss. Fucking legendary!" Rud replied with a howling laugh this time.

Chapter 3

Waking up with my head still ringing from my skull-rattling kiss with the glass wasn't going to stop me from feeling like a badass. Holding my head, I strutted out of our shack with quite the pep in my step to find Rud conversing with BJ.

"Well, if it isn't the human fighter himself. Put on quite the show yesterday. How are you feeling?" BJ asked.

"My head is fucking pounding, but mission accomplished, I guess," I replied with a giant smile on my face.

"I'd say you made my tag experience quite enjoyable, seeing that bloody mark on that human's face looking down at me. You also took two damn tags like a champ, and that gave me back some strength to look Jolene in the eye while I was getting mine. Appreciate you, lil' man. You would have made your Pops proud, and it goes without saying you made me just as proud!" BJ exclaimed.

"Not going to lie—I was out cold, so I didn't get to see it, but I'm happy to have been of service. You guys know what time it is, by the way? I'm starving, and there was no food at the door today."

Rud and BJ just shrugged.

"BJ, they've fed you every morning, have they not? Hopefully, my stunt last night didn't cause this."

"Every morning, like clockwork, really. I was just saying to Rud that I was surprised none of the humans had come in yet," BJ replied.

It was maybe another hour or so before the humans came, and they didn't bring food—they brought more fear.

They were dressed in long white coats with some blue cloth covering their faces, and their hands looked to be covered in some blue skin-like material. All three of the humans were there, and we could hear them talking about where they were going to start.

We watched as they went to the opposite wall of prisons and started grabbing rats out of their shacks and putting them in boxes. The majority had red-colored tags, which were different from our yellow-colored tags. I counted about twenty, but wasn't sure if I got them all. I saw that Goe the baker was one of them, though. After the boxes were full, they left the room and took the rats with them.

After about an hour or two, they returned with only half of the boxes and a black sack. They started to unload the boxes of rats back into their prisons, and I could only count around ten, and maybe less. Goe was still there, but he looked very disheveled, and was soaked in what I first thought was sweat. After a more thorough look, I saw that it seemed thicker, more like a clear, fatty substance or jelly. It covered all of them except for their snouts.

"Where are the rest of them? Did you guys recognize anyone who didn't come back?" I asked BJ and Rud.

"I saw Amy and her two nephews go, but none of them came back," Rud answered.

"It looked like they took Brando, and Ryco as well, but again, I didn't see them come back, either," BJ replied.

"Amy? Is that Hector's sister and his two kids she was fostering? Brando the janitor and Ryco the cart man?"

"Yes, that's them. Hopefully, they're okay," BJ replied. Then, his face went completely white and his eyes screamed fear.

Bob was putting one of the rats back when he turned to Jenny. "We have a late casualty."

Shaking his head, he grabbed the black sack from Jenny and put it on the ground, rolling back the opening to reveal its contents. It was full!

Piled in a heap, the rest of the rats that had been taken were there, and they were all dead! All of them were stiff as boards, covered in the jelly.

The man dropped the rat he was holding on top of the pile, rolled the bag back up, and left the room, followed closely by Jenny.

"Holy mother of cheesus, what the fuck!?" BJ yelled as I started to gag uncontrollably. Rud straight-up fainted the moment the body hit the pile. We could see all the other rats who were watching the horror show scurrying franticly and screaming bloody murder. It was an instant madhouse.

During the chaos, no one had noticed Jenny re-entering the room. She was carrying food in one arm and water in the other. Within a second of her being noticed, every prison went quiet and seemed empty as every single rat ran for their shacks to hide. We all knew full well they gave no protection, but it was more out of instinct to seek shelter than for safety.

"I'm really sorry; this isn't what I enjoy, but we need your help to flush out these systems for human use," she started saying as she put food in the survivors' prisons. "You don't know this, but the earth is dying, and you little brave souls are going to help us save humanity. This is more important than your lil' cute brains can understand, but truly, I'm sorry, and will be forever grateful to you all."

Beating on the glass, I tried to get her attention and yell back at her, praying with every word that she would turn around and understand me.

"What the fuck do you mean, 'little brave souls?' You killed them! You killed Brando, you killed Ryco, you killed women and children, for fucks' sake!"

"Tomorrow will be even tougher than today, but, if we did our jobs right and our thesis is correct, more of you will survive each step. I promise you, I'll do everything I can to get this right every step of the way so I can bring as many of you with us as possible. I truly am sorry. Now, eat up. You will need your strength," Jenny exclaimed.

"Can she really be apologizing right now, but saying in the next breath that it will only get worse? I don't understand how she can call herself a Momma and then go about killing the ones she refers to as kids. This is madness. This is insanity. Are humans really this vile?" I said to myself.

When she finished dumping the food into the prisons on the opposite wall, Jenny turned to head to our side. She finally noticed me pounding on the glass and came right up to the glass to look me in the eye.

"I'm sorry, lil' one. Did you know them? Or are you just hungry and know that I have food?" she said as her nose smushed into the glass.

"Of course I knew them! I grew up in the same damn town! You're a monster, a fucking monster!" I screamed.

"You must be hungry, since we didn't feed any of you today. Let me give you something a little extra for being such a smart little one," she said with a whisper, reaching into her food bag.

She was quick to drop the food as I jumped viciously at her hand, trying to latch on. I wanted so badly to get a hold of her hand and die trying to avenge my fallen townsfolk.

"Oh, yes—you're the feisty little one that Bob absolutely hates. Not going to lie, I hate Bob too, but you don't need to be like that to me. Remember, I'm Momma Jenny," she said as she put the screen back over my prison and went about finishing up with everyone else's food.

How sick is this lady? No mother would treat her kids like this. No mother would be so evil, I thought.

After she left the room, I took the food inside to Rud and Bissy. Rud was sitting up, completely white and in a daze. I don't even think he saw me come back into the shack.

"What happened out there, GW? I heard a lot of commotion, and Rud hasn't said a word or even acknowledged me. He's just been staring blankly at the wall since you brought him back in," Bissy asked.

"You don't want to know, Bissy, and to be honest, I don't even think I could even put it into words. All I know is, we need to get out of here, and fast. Help me lay Rud down, and then you should eat something before the lights go out."

I sat by the doorway for much of the night, but neither BJ nor anyone else, for that matter, came out of their shacks after Jenny left.

Rud never joined us to eat, as he fell asleep before we even sat down to eat. We sat in silence throughout dinner, and I, for one, was more than happy not to discuss what had just happened. I tried to stay up after reluctantly eating with Bissy, but it was nearly impossible.

My eyelids started to feel as heavy as dumbbells. Feeling like I couldn't fight it any longer, I retreated to bed and went to face my nightmares.

The nightmares were horrendous, and I woke up completely drenched with sweat. It felt like I hadn't slept for more than a few minutes, and my eyelids were just as heavy as when I had turned in.

Something wasn't right. I felt disoriented and sluggish, and my breathing was slow and labored. Trying to lift my hands to wipe the sleep from my eyes didn't work. My arms were paralyzed, and I couldn't even lift my head to look at them. I could only see Bissy lying beside me out of the corner of my eye.

I faintly saw someone walking into the shack, yet couldn't make out that it was Rud until he was standing directly over me. "GW, you okay, man?" Rud asked.

I can't speak. What's going on with me? I thought before it hit me: Rud hadn't eaten with us last night. Something must have been in the food!

My eyes started to glaze over, and all I could do was try to move them left to right to signal Rud that something was wrong. He didn't notice until he lifted my arm and watched it fall lifelessly back onto the bed.

"Shit, shit, shit," he said frantically as he leaned down to check my heartrate. Leaning over me, he pushed Bissy and got the same lifeless feeling. I could see the moment in his eyes when it clicked for him before he even said, "Fuck, the food!"

Trying to speak was almost impossible, but I was able to get out what was supposed to be, "Bury her." I could tell it wasn't much more than a grumble.

"What? What are you trying to tell me?" Rud replied.

Pointing my eyes at Bissy's limp body, I tried again and again. "Bbbbbbbb herrr. Bbbby herrrr."

After about the fourth or fifth time, I was exhausted, but he finally got me. Rolling Bissy off the bed, he started shoveling wood chips over her. Finishing it up by laying down on top of the mound to compact it and make it look slept-in, he turned to me and said, "They're back! The humans are back."

There was nothing I could do—no fighting or lashing out at them. I just had to lie there as the shack was pulled back.

It was Bob. He lifted me out and placed me in a box beside a bunch of other rats who all laid there lifelessly. "Looks like we're going to be short a few rats for this one. Not all of them ate last night," Bob said as he put the shack put back over top of Rud and Bissy.

The top of the box I was in closed, but, knowing that they were safe for now, the tiniest bit of relief came over me.

The relief didn't last, and it was replaced with fear as the box reopened. One by one, we were picked out and placed on a freezing-cold surface. It surprised me, as I hadn't felt anything since waking up this morning. Bob lifted my head and placed something over my nose and mouth, which instantly filled my lungs with more air than I had been able to intake in some time. It felt like I was no longer inhaling or exhaling, but being forced oxygen and then having it sucked back out of my lungs. It was incredibly painful at first, and, while my body quickly became used to it, my brain was rightfully confused.

After a few moments, Jenny came over, lifted me into a glass jar, and began to cover my body with the clear jelly that I had seen Goe soaked in the day before. It only took a few seconds before the entire jar was full, and my limp body was suspended, floating in a vat of jelly. The thing over my nose and mouth continued to push and pull air from my lungs as my eyes slowly started to regain focus and my neck started to relax. Turning my head to the right, I was able to see Jolene in the jar beside me, but I didn't recognize the man to my left.

The jelly was warm and thick. My body hadn't gained much function back, so escaping was impossible. My mind was racing with every forced breath. Was I going to die here like so many had yesterday? Would I see Mum, and maybe even Father again in the afterlife? No answers ever came, only question after question.

Minutes turned to hours as we floated there, and the longer it went on, the more my eyes fixated on Jolene. She hadn't opened her eyes once until suddenly, they shot open. They were completely bloodshot, red and filled with nothing but fear. She started convulsing, sending jelly spilling out the top of her jar onto the cold table as she shook more and more violently. It only lasted a few moments, but it seemed like she couldn't breathe—until she coughed. Her mask went completely red as it filled with blood, her eyes closed, and she went limp.

I could hear the man next to me start splashing around, doing the same, but I couldn't take my eyes off Jolene's lifeless body. I couldn't help her. I couldn't cry. I couldn't scream. I just had to sit there, watching her lifeless body float.

First Mum, now Jolene! Both my biological mother and the second mother who had helped raise me. *Why couldn't it have been me who fell? Why couldn't have been me who succumbed to this disgusting jelly?*

If there was a god, he definitely wasn't a rat. I must be cursed. There couldn't be any other reason why all this shit was happening to the ones I loved.

As I watched Bob pull Jolene out of the jar and throw her into the black sack of death, I knew the worst was yet to come for me. I would have to face BJ again…

Jenny went jar-by-jar, taking the survivors and putting us back into the box. Goe was there in the box when I arrived, and we embraced at first sight. I didn't know how many of us had been put in the box initially, but there were only nine of us who were put back in.

"I can't believe what's happening, GW! I can't believe what they're doing to us!" Goe sobbed. "These monsters, they're torturing us!"

"Humans, Goe. They're fucking humans—despicable creatures that believe they're doing this for their own good. That lady who calls herself Jenny admitted it to me. Can you believe she tried to apologize and say it was for the best?"

"I'm not going to lie, man. I don't think I can do this anymore. I would rather die at this point," Goe said as he continued to sob, squeezing me even tighter.

"I'm right there with you. As crazy as it sounds, I would trade places with Jolene in that black sack just so I don't have to look BJ in the eye."

Before Goe could reply, the box reopened, and Bob looked down at us, counting the survivors. "Odd number. Not as many as we were hoping, but still an odd number. Move on to Test Two without paralysis?" he said turning to Jenny.

"No, Test Two will have to be tomorrow. We don't have enough for a proper data run," she replied.

Shaking his head, Bob closed the box back up, and we could feel it lift off the ground. We were heading back to the prison, and the lump in my throat started to grow. With every jolting step Bob took, it grew larger and larger. I was praying that he would put me into a different prison just so I didn't have to face BJ.

As the box started to open again, I was met with yet another reminder that there was no god, or at least, not one who cared about my wishes or rats' lives.

Back into the same prison I went.

Chapter 4

By the time they put me back into my prison, it was well past nighttime, but Rud was sitting at the shack door waiting for me, and I could see BJ standing in his prison, looking over at Jolene's cell. I didn't dare lock eyes with him. I didn't even glance over. Still covered in the leftover jelly, I couldn't risk going to shower. I went straight inside the shack and got onto the bed.

I paid for my cowardice, though, as the wood chips that made up the bed stuck to me and caused me to scratch the hell out of myself. "Dude, go shower, man. This is disturbing to watch," Rud finally barked at me.

"I can't, man. I can't see BJ right now. I'm so disturbed and upset, I can't even begin to tell you what happened to me or what I had to watch."

"Do you want to talk about it? I obviously want to know what's happening, but your red eyes are making me question whether I really want to know," Rud replied.

"My eyes? What the hell are you talking about?"

"Shhh, man. Bissy is sleeping. She didn't take you getting taken too well—let alone freaking out over the paralysis," Rud whispered. "Your eyes are bloodshot to all hell, man. It's like all the blood vessels doubled in size, and I can barely even see any white left in them."

"Fuck. Not going to lie, that's the least of my worries. Can you do me a favor, man? Can you check if BJ is still up? I'm going to scratch the fur right off me and be completely red if I don't get this shit off."

Rud didn't even reply; he just got up and started walking towards the door. He stopped briefly and looked like he was going to say something, but then, deciding against it, continued walking. I figured he had a million questions, but I just wasn't ready to relive today, not knowing how he would take it or if I could even do it justice at this point. All I could think about was BJ and the incessant need to scratch my entire fur coat off.

"You're all clear, man. I can hear him crying away in there, and rightfully so, but I don't think he's coming back out anytime soon. I got the water bottle going for ya, but you might want to hurry up so you don't flood the place again," Rud said.

As I sat under the rushing water, Jolene's lifeless eyes staring into my soul kept popping into my brain. *I need to think of a way out of here. I can't watch anyone else go through this. Not Rud, and certainly not Bissy, let alone anyone else.*

What Rud said to me before I headed out to the shower hit me just before I took the wood chip out of the water bottle to end the flow: "Don't flood the place again."

That would definitely get us out of the glass prison, but that seemed to be the easiest part of the plan. After we got out would be when the real risk came into play—I didn't know what was beyond the door besides the jars of jelly and the ice-cold table, let alone how we would get off the table. All I knew was that we had to do something now, as anything would be better than going through another day of whatever the humans had planned for us.

I jammed the water bottle open again and ran back to the shack to discuss with Rud. "Rud, you still up?" I said as I came running back in, still sopping wet.

"Of course, man. You couldn't even dry off? What's going on?" he replied.

"We need to come up with a plan to escape, and I think I know where to start. Well, to be honest, I already started it. The water bottle is lodged open. We're flooding this bitch. We just have to figure out how to get off the table and out the door."

He shook his head and laughed. "You really think we can escape?"

"We have to fucking try, or we're all going to die in here. I've figured out the first part, now get your head in the game, and let's figure out the rest," I snapped back.

"Okay, okay, I feel you. Sorry. Can you dry off while we chat, though? Because it's hard to take you seriously standing there sopping wet," he replied.

I know he hadn't endured what I did today, but how could he make jokes at a time like this? It took everything in me not to punch him, but I wasn't going to let my anger get the better of me now. I had to remind myself that his ignorance wasn't his fault, nor was my deathly experience mine. If anyone needed to feel my anger, it was the humans—Mother of death Jenny, and Bob, the heartless Bob.

"Rud, I need another favor as I dry off: I need you to get BJ to flood his tank. Do not let him get you talking, and do not let him say no! Tell him to do it, and that's that."

"I don't know if he's going to answer, let alone listen to me, but I'll give it a shot," Rud replied.

I could hear him yelling at BJ as I started to dry off. "Just shut up! Fucking do it. Remember what you used to say to me when you would throw me in the drunk tank? 'You're worth more than this, so stop your sulking, and fucking be the man I know you are. You can live another day. You can live it differently.' Now is the time for me to say it to you! Just put the fucking wood chip in, and you can cry all you want afterwards."

I couldn't hear a response from BJ, or if there even was one, but Rud came back in and said he saw him wedge the bottle open and go back to his shack. I could tell Rud was rattled from having to do it, but I'm sure a part of him felt good about being able to give some hard love to the man who had never judged him during his darkest hours.

We stayed up the entire night, going back and forth on ideas, but none seemed to stick. The table was still getting in the way, and all we had for the door was squeezing under it. After that, it was nothing but wild theories about what was beyond. Time flew, and before we knew it, we were knee-deep in water, and Bissy was starting to stir.

"Bissy, how are you feeling?" I asked softly.

"The better question is, how are you? When did you get back?" she asked.

"Well, late last night, while you were sleeping, but there isn't any time for me to go into any detail. We're going to try and break out of here. We have flooded the place again, and Jenny should be in shortly to do the feeding. You going to be able to run when we need to?"

She caught me off-guard by looking at me with a smile, giving me the affirmative.

I knew Rud was also ready, but was I? I hadn't even taken the time to compute what had just happened to me, let alone to decide I was ready for this.

But I didn't have a choice but to be ready, because as soon as I started to question it, Jenny walked in.

"Are you kidding me? Again!" we could hear her say. "And another one. What the hell? We don't have time for this today."

She lifted off our soaked shack and verbally scolded us. "Do you realize how much I need to get done this morning, and now I have to add you and your damn neighbor to the list?"

The three of us just stared at her as if we had no idea what she was saying.

Off the shelf we went. She lifted us back out and onto the table, as she'd done the last time. This time, she didn't hesitate, and instantly put a box over us, only lifting it to place BJ in with us.

The first part of the plan had worked! I was shocked.

"Alright, you got me here. What's next?" BJ asked the moment the box closed.

"To be honest, BJ, this is as far as the plan got us. We can try and push the box over the edge and hope it braces our fall, but that's all we've really got," Rud replied, as I still couldn't even look BJ in the eye, let alone answer him.

"Are you goddamn fucking kidding me?" he yelled. "I knew you three needed me. Listen up. As soon as this box lifts even slightly, I need you to run right at her and use her clothes as your way down."

"Like, you mean you want us to climb down her?" Bissy asked.

"Yes, that's exactly what I want you to do. I'm going for revenge; you go for safety!" he replied.

"BJ, you can't—" I started to say before he again cut me short, as he normally did.

"Yes, I fucking do. They took Jolene and David from me, and I want to take a piece of this human with me. Do not try and stop me. When this box tilts, you run right at her. End of story. Get ready!" BJ said with such aggression that none of us even tried to challenge him.

We didn't have to wait long. The moment we saw even the slightest light come from under an edge, we ran for it, pushing it up and rushing out into the light, all four of us screaming at the top of our lungs, so loud that even Jenny looked like she was more scared then surprised. She didn't have time to get up from her chair.

Pulling in front of the group, BJ leaped onto her hand and ran straight up her arm towards her face while the other three of us slid down her long white coat towards the floor. We could hear BJ cursing and screaming his wife's name behind us, but we were on the floor and headed towards the door before we turned around and saw him latched onto one of her ears. She was thrashing around while he scratched at her face, opening cut after cut with every turn of her head.

We were about to slide under the door when Bob whipped it open and ran for Jenny, almost crushing Rud and myself in the process. The door shut with us on the other side of it.

BJ had succeeded, but we knew what the cost was shortly after the door closed. We heard Jenny stop screaming, and as we turned back towards the door, we were met a bone-crushing thud against it that caused us all to jump back. We saw the blood start to run out from under the door and we knew it was BJ who had caused the horrific noise. There was nothing we could do for him except continue to run.

We were in a giant hallway with too many doors to count. It was incredibly bright, with nowhere for us to hide. Our only hope was to check each door and see if there was one that lead out of this white-walled hell.

"Which door? There are so many," I said, looking at Rud.

"I don't know, man! Bissy, you pick!" Rud replied.

Bissy shrugged, as she was still fixated on the pool of blood on the floor, which continued to grow from under the door. There was no time to argue; the decision of which door was made for us, as it sounded like Bob and Jenny were heading for the door behind us.

"They're coming! Closest one it is!" I said before squeezing under it, followed immediately by the other two.

The room was cold and dark, but we were not alone, as we could hear rustling, clanking, and numerous things breathing on the walls beside us.

It was only a matter of seconds before we were noticed, and something spoke. "What are you fine things doing in here? Come closer, so I can get a better look at you. My eyes are bad, and it's far too dark in here, with the lights being off and all." There was an elegant-yet-mischievous tone to its voice.

Attempting to deepen my voice to hopefully make myself seem larger, I replied, "Who are you? More importantly, where and what are you?"

"My name is Trix, and I'm in the cage to the right. Come a few steps forward so I can see who I'm talking to," the voice replied.

As I started to step forward, a deep, old voice came out of the cage to the left and made me think twice. "I wouldn't do that if I were you. He can see you all too well, and any closer, and you will be her lunch. He is a feline, after all."

"Don't you listen to that old dog," Trix replied, and this time, there was no elegance, only the mischievousness.

Dog? I had only heard about them in an old children's book in the school library. The book told a tall tale of a rat befriending a dog and how that dog had carried the rat on his back as they travelled, keeping the rat safe from felines and hawks. It was quite the tale, but I sure as hell had never seen any dogs.

"I appreciate that advice. What's your name? I personally have never seen a dog in my short years, but I read a story about a rat and a dog being close friends once," I asked the dog.

"Ah. I, too, heard a story like this when I was younger," the dog exclaimed before its voice became a tad frantic. "I can hear the humans outside; they're about to check in here for you. I can introduce myself after, but you guys may want to jump in here. You can hide behind me for now," the dog proclaimed.

Rud didn't even question it; he jumped into the cage on the left and helped Bissy in without hesitation. The bars were wide enough that we were able to slip right through, with no tucking tummies or licking fur.

I guess we're doing this. Trusting a voice in the dark from an animal we have never seen before. Interesting, I thought.

Trix started going nuts as the door opened, making that horrific meowing sound that we used to hear in the forest above Tails Falls. He was trying to alert the humans that we were in the cage beside him.

"He stole my lunch. Why did you put me in here with that old, smelly piece of four-legged garbage?" Trix meowed, but to no avail.

Before the light reached the cage, the old dog swept me under his chest with a massive fur-covered paw. It was the warmest and most comforting feeling I had felt in days.

"My name is Tex," he whispered. "You're a trusting one. You got lucky this time, and I would advise against that in the future. You never know who you're dealing with. Trust should be earned, not blindly given. You may not get this lucky next time."

Bob and Jenny stepped through the door, flooding the whole room with light. Peeking out from under Tex's paw, I could see the two checking under the table and behind the boxes on the adjacent wall. The room wasn't much different than the glass prison-lined one that we had just escaped from—just replace the glass prison-covered walls with walls of barred cages that imprisoned dogs and cats instead of rats. The same style desk was in between, and the same stench of despair lingered in the air.

"Trix, can you shut up already? You're the most annoying cat, not to mention a disgustingly ugly one. At this rate, you're going to get sent back for another round of injections if you keep this shit up," Bob said, kicking Trix's cage door with his foot.

The two humans checked high and low, but not in the cages. I'm sure they couldn't fathom that we would have jumped into a cage with a dog ten or fifteen times our size. They looked frazzled, and I could see the still very fresh and bloody scrapes on Jenny's cheeks. The room was dead quiet besides Trix's sulking after his cage got rattled.

None of the other inhabitants dared to make a single noise, or even got up to survey what the humans were doing. I wasn't even sure if a few of them were even alive, as they were still as rocks in the forest.

It didn't take long before Bob and Jenny moved on to the next room, and as soon as the door shut, the room came to life. The rocks stretched and revealed their animal features. The dogs went straight back to lying down, while the cats circled their cages, taunting Trix for his ability to bring attention to himself. It was quite the experience to see felines up close while being completely safe on the other side of the bars, let alone being protected and hidden by a dog.

"Tex, my name is GW. The other two are Bissy and Rud. It's an absolute honor to meet you, and I'll heed your warnings on trust. We didn't see much of a choice here. We escaped from the prison across the hall, and are looking for a way out of here. I assume you wouldn't know one, would ya?"

"Well, to be honest, no and yes. The last time I was out there must have been years ago now. I've been in here for so long I've lost count of the months, or even years. Don't even bother with the rest of them in here, either. All of them were born here. I'm the only dog left in here who has ever felt the gloriousness of grass in his paws and wind in his fur."

He stopped and looked like he went deep into thought, as if he was remembering himself outside. At least, the glimmer of light in his eyes, which certainly wasn't there before, made me think so.

He continued. "If my memory hasn't failed me completely, it's either the third or fourth door on the right. The one with the red box beside it."

Seeing that light in Tex's eye made me want to bring him with us, but I knew there was no way he was getting under the door, and we were all way too small to open it. Such a kind, gentle beast didn't deserve to be locked up like this. For fuck's sake, none of these animals did, even Trix.

I could feel the anger building again, which was a good thing, as Tex's comforting presence had made the adrenaline start to fade. We needed to get moving before we got complacent.

"GW, you guys better get moving. The humans are at least a few doors down by now, but they should be back to feed us shortly," Tex spoke as if he could read my mind.

"Before we go, do you want me to open the cage? I know you can't get under the door like we can, but it's the very least we could do," I asked.

"To be honest, having some company other than that whining feline has been more than enough payment," Tex replied with that same glimmer of light in his eye.

Trix heard him and made sure he knew it. "Fuck off, old dog. I'm going to be a hell of a lot worse now. You cost me far more than just a meal."

Tex chuckled and gave us a wink. "Go on now! Go get your freedom!"

Rud and I slid through the bars and down on to the floor. Turning to help Bissy down, we saw her lean in and kiss Tex right on his big wet nose. "We can't thank you enough, sir. You are a gentleman," Bissy said as she wiped her lips and reached for our hands.

If Tex's fur weren't a golden shade of light brown, I would have sworn he was bright red from blushing. Leave it to Bissy to make an old dog blush. To give him some extra satisfaction, we waved goodbye to Trix before turning to give him a wink of our own.

Slipping under the door and back into the bright, sterile hallway brought back a rush of adrenaline that pulsated through my entire body. From head to tail, I could feel the anxiety and fear return. My hands went instantly sweaty as my eyes darted around from door to door, looking for the red box on the wall.

We darted to the right side of the hallway and ran as fast as we could, counting the doors as we went. Stopping at the third door, we looked up to see the red box, but it was right in the middle between the third and fourth door. *Fuck. He didn't say if it was on the right or the left of the door.*

"Right or left, third or fourth?" Rud pressed.

"Tex was to the left, so I say we go left to the fourth door," Bissy replied.

It wasn't like her to give an opinion or suggestion for that matter. Rud and I weren't going to take away her newfound voice, so we just nodded in agreement. "The fourth door it is," we agreed.

Bob must have spotted us as we slid under the door, because we could hear him yell for Jenny. "They just went into the pigeon room!"

Their footsteps echoed down the empty hallway as they ran towards us.

We found ourselves looking around for an exit that wasn't there. We had picked the wrong door, and there was no time to retreat and go back to the third door. We were trapped, and there was no Tex to save us this time.

"I'm sorry, guys. I should have kept my mouth shut, like I always do," Bissy pouted.

"Don't even. To be honest, I was thinking the same thing," Rud replied.

"Back away from the door, guys. Our only chance is to rush out the moment they open it and try for the other door."

Backing up a few steps, we all crouched as if we were about to run track at school. The door opening was the gong to start the race, and we bolted. Rud was the first one to reach Jenny, and he easily passed her as she stepped into the room. Bissy and I narrowly dodged her grasp by veering in opposite directions, which caused both of us to lose some of our forward momentum, and slowed me just enough for Jenny to step on the tip of my tail with her foot.

Rud turned to look at me as I screamed in pain. Distracted, he ran full-tilt straight into Bob's open hands. He was scooped up, and simultaneously, I felt the tip of my tail give way, sending me tumbling forward, leaving streaks of blood behind me as my broken tail flung around. Before I could regain my footing, Bob was there to grab me with his other hand.

Both Rud and I tried fighting, but Bob's grip was so tight that I felt my rib cage compressing. The pressure increased 'til it felt like my ribs were going to cave in any second, and my vision went dark from the pain. When the pressure started to subside, and my vision started to return, I was met with the sight of a teary-eyed Bissy being held by Jenny.

My eyes welled up at the sight. Our escape had failed.

Chapter 5

"Bob, why is this female not tagged?" Jenny said with a very disappointed tone in her voice.

"What? There's no way. I measured and tagged every single one," Bob replied.

"You most certainly didn't. This little girl came from the same tank as these other two. The one you threw at the door was from the other one—both tanks you tagged and signed off on!" Jenny replied, but with a far sharper disciplinary tone this time.

Bob looked right at me and whispered angrily, "You're the bane of my life, you know that, right?"

"Don't blame the rat. You sound like a child. Put them back in their cage, and I'll figure out how we'll deal with this one. We can't have her skewing the data points now," Jenny snarked.

We could hear Tex and the other dogs howling as we passed their door. They must have heard that we had been caught. Knowing that even after Tex's help and BJ's bravery and sacrifice, we still failed, made the trek back down the hallway even more heartbreaking.

Actually, *I* failed. It was my idea, after all. Not only that, I didn't know what the two humans meant about skewed data points, but it certainly didn't sound good for Bissy. I was the reason she didn't have tags, so whatever happened, again, it was on my shoulders.

The door to our penitentiary was open, and all the rats were standing up against their glass walls as we entered. Every one of them was silent, staring at us. The only one that showed any emotion was Goe. He caught my gaze as he dropped to his knees, hands screeching down the glass as tears rolled down his cheeks.

If I weren't feeling dead inside, I probably would have cared what he was feeling. I would have tried to show him it would be okay. But after this, it wasn't going to be okay, and I couldn't deny that any longer.

Bob placed Rud and I back into the same glass box we had called jail for the past few days, while Jenny placed Bissy alone in BJ's old cell. I watched as Rud ran over to the glass and placed his hands against Bissy's.

I should have felt anything but anger, but it was anger that took me over—anger at myself. I may have had Rud for company, but the only company I wanted now was self-loathing.

Bissy and Rud stayed beside each other all night, while I went into our old shack and built myself a bed to lie on and blame myself. "How could you think that you could escape this? After all that you've caused, you thought you would be a hero?" I asked myself out loud. "You really thought you could get out of this hell and bring them with you? Save Bissy from tagging and the horrors of the jelly? How naïve and stupid you are."

As the night went on, my hunger and the exhaustion from defecating on my soul started to play tricks on me. I must have fallen asleep without knowing, as BJ walked into the shack. "You said you would look after David for me," he said.

He was then replaced by my father. "I told you to follow in my footsteps and keep everyone safe, especially your mother." Before I could reply, he left.

I cried until my mother came into focus, and, to my surprise, she walked right over to my bedside. She smiled at me, leaned over, and kissed me on my forehead, whispering into my ear as she used to when I would get myself in trouble. "You shouldn't judge yourself on your actions of yesterday, but how you handle yourself tomorrow. Be strong, be yourself, and you will be better. You will survive."

I lunged to try and hug her, but was woken up by falling straight off the bed onto the floor. It had felt so real. Why couldn't that last part have been real?

I cried myself back to sleep, my self-loathing replaced by the hole in my heart from missing my mother, and unfortunately—or fortunately—the nightmares didn't return.

I slept almost the entire next day, only awakening when the humans in their white coats returned with a few rats from their daily slaughter. It must have been the red tags' turn, as I only saw them returning, and most of the rats I had seen staring at us when we returned from our failed escape were still there, staring up at me. "What the fuck are they looking at? Are they angry we left without them? Are they sad we were caught? Gah, stop staring at me," I angrily said to myself under my breath.

Rud interrupted my inner turmoil and offered his take as he walked over from talking to Bissy. "I don't think they know what to make of us, or they're struck with wonder about what happened. I've been trying not to look at them, cause, to be honest, it's creeping me the hell out," he said with a subtle chuckle.

I was taken aback again by his humor, but couldn't help but chuckle in agreement.

"What happened to you last night? You were screaming something awful in there, and then you just started balling. I wanted to come and check on you, but, honestly and selfishly, I didn't want to leave Bissy's side," Rud continued.

"A whole lot of self-loathing and terrible nightmares, man. Not going to lie, I needed the space, so thank you. What did I miss today? How many?"

"How many made it back? I think five out of the twenty who left. None of them came back with the jelly on them this time, though, so that was different," he replied, slowly peeking over his shoulder at Bissy.

I was a little taken aback by the numbers, but couldn't help but notice the glance back at Bissy. "How is she holding up?" I asked.

"No sugar-coating—she is terrified, and I don't know what to even say to her. You know her; she doesn't speak much, but she blames herself for us being caught. She isn't listening to me. You want to give it a try while I go try and wash my own emotions away in the shower?" he asked.

Nodding, I gave him a fist bump, took a deep breath, and started over to Bissy. She was sitting with her back to the glass, hunched over, just staring at her hands. Her black-and-white coat was tattered in a way I wasn't used to seeing, even from myself or any of the other boys in town. She was always so well-groomed that her fur always had a shine like no one else's. It hurt even to see her in that state, let alone the pain I felt for what she was experiencing mentally.

I tried tapping on the glass, but she wouldn't turn to face me, so I pushed my back against the glass behind hers and sat down. "Bissy, I don't even know where to start. You can't blame yourself; you didn't cause this. If anyone is to blame, it's me. I put us in that situation. I told Rud to have BJ join us. I should've had a better plan," I said as I found myself staring at my own hands.

She still didn't reply, so I continued. "Come on, Bissy. It was a fifty-fifty shot, and I would've picked the same as you. How could any of us have known that they would see us right at that moment? We could have chosen the other door and still been caught, they had seen us at that point."

There was no reply.

What else can I even say? I wondered.

I was about to continue when she screamed.

I whipped around to see Jenny's hand around Bissy as she pulled her out of her prison. Jenny was dressed in her white coat with the blue gloves and mask on. My heart sank.

Upon hearing Bissy's blood curdling scream, Rud shot over to me like a bat out of hell, knocking me over as he hit the glass in full stride. "Noooooooooooooo!" he screamed as his legs went limp and he fell to the ground beside me.

We both couldn't take our eyes off Bissy as she was put down on the table. At first, I thought she was going to get measured and tagged, but Jenny didn't go for the drawer. Instead, reaching into her coat pocket, she grabbed a long tube with a needle on the end. It was filled with some sort of red liquid, and as she stuck the needle into Bissy's neck and pressed down on the tube with her thumb, the liquid emptied.

"What the hell is that? What are they doing to her!?" Rud yelled two millimeters from my face as he shook me violently. I had no answers, and I was just as angry as he was, but I couldn't say or do anything as he continued to shake me, shouting, "I'm going to kill that bitch, I tell ya. I am going to kill her!"

As quickly as the horror started, it ended. I could swear I saw Jenny lean over and whisper something into Bissy's ear before placing her back into her prison and walking out of the room. Bissy was visibly disoriented; she swayed back and forth as she made her way over to the glass ,where Rud and I were both trying to break through to her. Rud was speaking a mile a minute, frantically trying to figure out if Bissy was okay.

"I don't know. There are four of you guys. Can you stop beating on the glass?" Bissy replied, trying to stabilize herself on the glass.

I interrupted Rud with my hand in front of his face. "Sit down, Bissy. Please," I said, trying to keep my voice calm.

She didn't reply, but plopped herself down with a thud. Her eyes were not her regular blue; they were glassy, and seemed to be turning a shade of green right in front of us. The whites of her eyes were as pure white as my fur, and I couldn't see a single blood vessel in them. It was incredibly odd.

"Bissy, what did she say to you?" I inquired.

"Something about her being sorry and hoping to see me tomorrow," she replied before turning to Rud. "Rud. If something happens to me, I wanted to ask you to tell my mother and brother that I love them. I appreciate everything you've done for me. You took me by surprise with your kindness and care. You brought me out of my shell. You truly are a great man—the man of my dreams, you could say."

Rud burst into tears and pressed his hands against the glass where she had hers. Not wanting to ruin the moment, I quietly got up, put a hand on Rud's shoulder, and slowly walked away. I should have seen this coming. I had seen them whispering to each other on the trail that dreadful night we were first taken, not to mention the care Rud took in helping hide Bissy from everything and them spending the night together after our failed escape. I felt stupid for not putting two and two together sooner. He wasn't that much older than us, and she'd always seemed older than her years, so if we had made it out, I could have seen them making a great couple. The storybooks always had happy endings to these types of stories, but I couldn't see how this could be the case this time.

Food was delivered shortly after I left, but I didn't want to disturb them, so I cautiously ate a small portion and left the remainder for Rud. At this point, I didn't even care if they had poisoned the food, as it had been more than a day since we last ate, and I was famished.

Sitting there alone on my bed, chomping away on a carrot, my mind started to wander. I used to love when it did that, but lately, it had only sent me to dark places.

My brain surprised me this time by taking me back to camping with David and BJ. It was one of my favorite weekend activities, and I started to imagine the food was one of Jolene's famous hard-cheese niblets. Sitting around the fire, we would all chomp them down while listening to BJ's stories about the adventures he and my father had been on.

One of my favorites was about the time my dad got his tail stuck in a door because he was too busy watching my mother walk by. He ended up tearing the tip of his tail off as he tried to go and introduce himself, which sent him tumbling into her, knocking them both to the ground and ruining my mother's finest dress. She was beside herself with anger until she noticed his bleeding tail and rushed him to my grandparent's house to bandage him up.

My dad always said he did it on purpose, but BJ knew it was a stroke of dumb luck, as my mother was way out of my father's league. BJ used to laugh and tell me my father would buy her fancy dresses every few months to try and wipe his guilt away for ruining her favorite dress. "Your dad was so scared by the look in her eye that day after she noticed her dress was ruined that he wanted to replace that memory by seeing her eyes light up over a new one. The poor guy almost went broke over that damn dress," he would say to finish the story.

My wandering mind was interrupted by the pain of my own torn tail, and it made me feel good to remember that my dad's tail looked the same. Now, if I ever lost his hat, I would always have my torn-ass tail to remember him by.

Luckily, the next day, I wasn't met with paralysis, although I was incredibly groggy from staying up too late thinking about campfire stories and trying not to itch my tail scab. I grabbed the leftover food to bring to Rud and headed out of the shack. The lights in the room were still off, and it was dead quiet, as none of the other rats had awoken yet. It was almost pitch-dark but I could make out a figure sitting up, so I assumed Rud was awake, but as I approached, I could hear him snoring away. It was too dark for me to see Bissy, and, seeing as Rud was still asleep, I left the meal a few steps from him and went to take a shower to try and wake myself up.

It was the wake-up I needed, and as I was drying off, I could see Rud stirring and wiping his eyes. He noticed the carrot and smelled it over and over. Obviously, unlike me, he was more worried than hungry, so I gave him a whistle to get his attention. After giving him a thumbs-up, he almost ate the thing whole. He was just as hungry, then, which gave me a good laugh to start the day.

Sadly, that was the last laugh I would have today, as the door opened shortly after, and all three of the humans came in with their death attire on.

There was no time for me to check on Bissy, as Jenny went straight for her cage and took her out of the room in a box by herself. Rud and I were quickly grabbed by Bob and placed in a box with a bunch of other yellow tags. We didn't say a word to each other as we bounced around and stumbled over each other with every footstep.

Before we reached our destination, we stumbled right into Joey and Bissy's mother. Rud grabbed them both without hesitation in a giant hug that had Joey staring at me with a very perplexed look on his face, which turned to sadness in two seconds flat when Rud spoke. "Bissy loves you. She loves you both so much." The three of them broke down into tears.

I couldn't even bring myself to go over and hug them, as I didn't want to feel anything. I didn't want to become any weaker than I already was, knowing what the jelly might hold for them, and even me for that matter. Looking at them, I tried to convince myself that I didn't even know them. *Do not cry, do not break; you need your strength, and you do not want to go through another Jolene.*

Bob cautiously peered into the box as he slowly pulled its flaps back. I thought he may be scared of me biting him again or some of us escaping, but, hearing Jenny yell at him to hurry up, I realized it was her he feared—the mother of death.

One by one, they started taking us out, and to my surprise, there were no glass jars in sight when I was finally lifted out of the box. There was, however, one of the needle devices waiting for me, but instead of the red liquid that had been given to Bissy the night before, it was filled with a green syrup-looking substance. I had wondered why we hadn't been poisoned, and this was the answer.

The moment the needle broke the skin on the back of my neck, and I felt the liquid start to enter my body. It slowly made me lose feeling starting in my neck, then in my arms, and, as it slowly crept down my spine towards my feet, the breathing mask was put on. My brain didn't panic this time, as it had felt the sensation of oxygen being forced in and out of my lungs only a few days prior.

Instead of being put into a jar, I was lowered into one of maybe twenty small metal coffins. It was lined with what looked to be cushions, and was surrounded by blinking red and green lights. After laying me down, Bob tucked the hose that was attached to my air mask behind my right ear and slid a pair of black goggles over my eyes. At first, everything was almost pitch-black, but as Bob closed the lid over top of me, the goggles lit up with an intense brightness that made my eyes burn. After a few blinding white flashes, they went clear, and once again, I could see the lights of the coffin blinking around me.

Fear started to creep in, and I couldn't help but wonder what the fuck was going to happen. However, I was feeling a bit of relief knowing that whatever happened, I wouldn't have to watch anyone else go through it or, worse yet, succumb to it.

Many minutes passed, and just as I could no longer distract myself by counting my forced breaths, there was a feeling of extreme pressure in both my arms and legs. Shooting pains fired throughout my entire body from head to tail. It only lasted a few excruciating seconds, and it ended with the goggles buzzing before going dark again.

Did I fall asleep? Am I dreaming? How am I outside right now? I thought.

I was standing in a meadow of swaying green grass, just a few steps away from a beautifully still pond. I could feel the grass brushing against my legs, and the warm breeze filled my nostrils with the soothing scent of spring flowers. It was instant bliss, and it caught me off-guard as dreams never felt this real.

Walking over to the pond and onto the warm sand was unlike anything I had ever experienced. It was so soft and fine, unlike the hard, clayish sand of the beach above Tails Falls, where David and I used to skip rocks and look for sea monsters. Looking around the shoreline, I noticed that all the rocks were almost perfectly round, flat, and begging to be skipped. My childish instinct kicked in, and I reached down for a rock to throw, but it was then that the dream went completely sideways.

I stopped an inch from the rock as I finally caught a glimpse of my hand. It was huge and furless. It wasn't the hand of a rat—it wasn't my hand! It was a human hand!

Bringing both of my hands up to my face and flipping them over and back again, I was in awe. It was fascinating to see and even feel the lines and crevices that covered my palms. The perfectly rounded nails and tiny hairs around my knuckles were so soft, unlike my real hands, with their sharp nails and coarse fur-covered backs.

Moving my attention from my furless meat mitts, I looked down and lifted my feet out of the sand, feeling each grain fall between my toes. *Are these what human feet look like? They're so odd, with their stubby toes that pale in comparison to their fingers.*

None of it made any sense, but before I could question my appearance any further, a shooting pain exploded from my temples down to my toes. My vision started to falter, as if I had been punched in the face and was losing consciousness.

This dream world was so real I had forgotten where I had been only a few short moments before—lying paralyzed in a metal box with a machine breathing for me. The reality sure set back in quickly, though, as the blackness faded, and again, I found myself unable to move. The blinking red and green lights were all I could see.

Holy hell, was that ever a dream! I would have called it a nightmare, if it weren't so real. How utterly fascinating was that? To spend a few moments in human skin? Unbelievable.

Not long after coming back to reality, I was startled when the lid to the metal box made a hissing sound and popped itself open. The pressure in my arms and legs returned, and it felt like numerous pins were being pulled out of my skin at the same time. Bob was there and, quickly taking off my goggles, he left the breathing machine over my snout as he lifted me out of the casket. I tried to survey the other boxes, but it looked as if they had all been opened and emptied. It was then that my brain shot back into fear and panic mode.

Was Rud okay? Were Bissy's mother and brother okay? What about Bissy? *Please tell me they're all okay! Please!*

My panic intensified as they put me into a small box all by myself.

There's no way I'm the only one! There's no way I'm the only one who lived!

When Bob returned to remove my breathing machine, I went into full-blown panic mode, and no longer having a regulated breathing pattern made it impossible not to succumb to the anxiety. As he lifted me back out of the box, he spoke to me as if he knew what I was thinking. "Alright. Not so feisty this time, eh? Guess we can get you back to your friends now."

I couldn't believe my ears, and even though I said I was done with tears, there was no fighting it. I broke down the second I saw Rud. He was hunched over with his head between his knees, but he didn't need to look up—I knew it was him. As the box lid closed and darkness fell over us, I sat down beside him and put my arm around his shoulders. He was visibly shivering, and, knowing how I'd felt after my time in the jelly, I didn't say a word. I just held him as we jolted around on our walk back to our cell, trying to listen to what the humans were talking about.

"That went a lot better than expected. We only lost one-third, and half of those were due to human error," Bob said.

"Definitely a remarkable improvement over the original oral ingestion tests. We'll have to look closer at the use of the BA-1 injectable serum for physical sedation in conjunction with the AR-2 serum for mental cognition during sleep cycles. I didn't think we would have that much success with BA-1, so it will be interesting to see how the female reacts to the BA-0," Jenny replied.

Is the BA-1 serum the green stuff they injected us with? And the BA-0 is what Bissy got? I pondered as they continued.

"We still have to see how the injectable serum holds up over the longer sleep cycles when it's mixed with the forced nutrition. I honestly think that's going to be the hardest part. We're going to have to regulate both the amount of serum needed and at what intervals—do we even have time for that? Aren't we supposed to move to human trials in a month or so?" Bob asked.

"Yes. We're going to have to accelerate our test schedules. Not only are human trials fast approaching, but the government also wants to have the first vessel leave Earth by the end of the year! It's madness, but you've seen the state of the planet. It's deteriorating faster than any of us predicted!" Jenny exclaimed.

Are they really going to do this to their fellow people after they're done with us? How sick are humans to not only do this to another species, but to themselves!? I was outraged, but I couldn't understand what they were talking about when it came to vessels. *Like, are they talking about boats? And how would they leave earth on a boat? These two are nuts!*

All that aside, the most troubling part of this conversation was the sentence, "We're going to have to accelerate our test schedules." How was that possible? They had been killing rats every day since we arrived here.

There had to be less than a hundred of us left out of the possibly three hundred that we originally estimated.

Overhearing this conversation raised more questions than it answered, but I wasn't sure if Rud had heard any of it. He never took his head out of his knees the whole walk back, let alone acknowledge me being there.

Upon arriving back at our cell, we were met by another new shack and a fresh meal piled up at the door. The fresh array of greens and carrots smelled delicious, and my appetite returned the moment I saw them.

Rud went straight over to the wall adjacent to Bissy's cell, but there was no sign of her. He still refused to look me in the eye, but he did help me drag the food into our shack and set up a spread for the both of us. We sat in silence as we ate, and my brain couldn't stop bouncing between my experience of human hands and wondering if Bissy was okay. There was still no sign of her, and we hadn't seen any of the humans come back into the room since returning us.

The silence and suspense were killing me. I had to talk, even if Rud didn't answer. "Did you hear what they were saying on our walk back?" I asked.

He was standing at the door, staring at Bissy's shack. "Do you think she's in there sleeping? She has to be, right? Her brother and mother, how can I tell her that they didn't come back with us?" he replied, completely ignoring my question. The last line hit me hard, how had I not noticed that they were not in the box with us? No wonder he was so distraught, fuck!

"I don't know, Rud, but I hope she is. I hope she's cuddled up fast asleep, dreaming of you." I said, trying my best to focus on Bissy and not her family.

He didn't take his gaze off her shack until I said, "dreaming of you."

Then, he wiped his eyes, turned to face me, and said, "Sorry, GW, I didn't answer your question. You know, I did hear what they were saying, and I'm not looking forward to the next few days." He turned his gaze back to her shack.

"Do you want to discuss what happened today or what?" I asked.

"What? The fact that I was made into a rat accordion when that breath machine started, or that after being put to sleep, I dreamt I was human?" he retorted.

The "rat accordion" part made me break out into laughter, and all I could get out was, "Rat accordion."

"You like that one, eh? It was the first thing I thought of after my initial fear subsided. You know me; I got to find some humor in things. Human hands are ridiculous, too. Huge meat sticks for fingers, with no fur to cover their awkward-looking knuckles," he replied.

If I wasn't in hysterics over his initial comment, I definitely was after the "meat sticks" comment. We both sat there laughing for a good ten to fifteen minutes until the lights went out, and we started to hear yelling and screaming coming from the wall across from us and even a few cells below us.

We thought the humans had come back, but as we went out, we could see a few rats yelling at what seemed to be nothing. The yells didn't seem to make any sense, and they were sporadic in nature, starting with only a handful, and growing to maybe fifteen or so rats holding their heads and yelling at the top of their lungs.

It got so loud that even the humans came in to see what was going on. As they entered the room and the lights went back on, a few rats fell over and stopped yelling instantly, but it seemed to amplify the angst of the majority.

"What the fuck is going on? Are they having a reaction to the BA-1 wearing off?" Bob asked Jenny, putting his face up to one of the cells.

Jenny was looking into another cell. She replied, "No, that would have been a while ago at this point. They're holding their heads; it must be overstimulation from the augmented reality serum and the experience itself. It looks like all of them are red tags, so it's only the ones grown in the lab. I can only assume they're having a hard time handling a reality they've never experienced. None of them will have felt real wind or any of the smells, as they all grew up in a sterile environment."

Bob was moving on to the next cell when the rat in the cell he'd started with began to bang its head against the glass violently. The brown-and-white rat looked to be in complete agony, its yelling having turned into a grotesque gurgle with foam erupting from its mouth.

It continued to slam its head harder and harder into the glass. *Thump, thump, thump.* You could see the white on its head beginning to go red as it split the top of its scalp open, smearing blood on the glass and still increasing the pace. It was disturbing to see its skull starting to give in before I could look away. The blood was gushing out at that point, and with one more excruciatingly loud scream, it lurched back and smashed its head against the glass with so much force that it made Bob fall back on the floor, gagging, as did Rud and I.

The rat had killed itself right in front of us by literally bashing its own brains out.

"Holy fuck! Are you fucking kidding me?" Bob finally got out after almost vomiting all over the floor.

Jenny helped him back to his feet and peered at the apparent suicide in disgust. "Well, that was disturbing," she exclaimed as she grabbed the cell from the wall and took it out of the room.

It was almost impossible to sleep that night. Not only was it horrifying to watch, but we could also hear it happening repeatedly throughout the night. *Thump, thump, thump, gargle. Thump, thump, thump, gargle.*

It happened over and over again, breaking for silence after the last loud thud, only to be replaced when the next rat decided to take its life.

It was a night one could only describe as bloody horrific.

Chapter 6

Sick to my stomach and rotten to my core is the only way I could explain how I felt after such a night.

We didn't dare leave the shack until Bob and Jenny came in to see the mess that they had created. Bob's squeamish stomach could barely take it, and even the Mother of Death seemed to be horrified by the scene.

"Bob, this is disgusting. Not a single red tag made it through the night. The poor little guys bashed their own brains out. I can't imagine what they were going through to do such an insane thing," Jenny said to Bob as he gagged, clearly trying to keep himself from vomiting. "Take the tanks out of the room. We'll have to clean them thoroughly before reusing them for future experiments."

"I don't know if I can stomach it. This isn't just disgusting; this is revolting," Bob replied before grabbing a tank and taking it out of the room.

After an hour or so, Bob returned one last time and said the words I was hoping we wouldn't hear today. "Now all that's out of the way, are we starting up today's experiment?"

"Yes. Get the containers powered up, and I'll get the BA-1 shots ready," Jenny replied without hesitation.

I turned to look at Rud, expecting him to be as fearful as I was, but he just winked at me and said, "You ready to get our accordion on and be human again, my friend? I know *I'm* kind of excited to feel furless again." He broke into a fit of laughter.

"How you find this funny is kind of beyond me, but, to be honest, I'm also kind of excited to feel like…what did you call them again? 'Meat sticks!?' That BA garbage can fuck right off, though," I replied, almost disgusted with myself.

"There you go! Isn't it nice finding the positives in the sick and twisted world we've been forced to endure?" he replied.

It didn't take long before we were being rounded up for our daily torture, but this time, neither Rud nor I fought it.

How desensitized have we become to actually be looking forward to this? I wondered curiously.

Goe was in the box as we were thrown in, but unlike us, he wasn't smiling. It was evident that he wasn't of the same mind as us.

"Did you guys see what happened last night? I couldn't sleep after that horror show, and the noises… my lord, the noises—" Goe started before Rud raised a hand to interrupt him.

"Goe, I love you, man, and yes, that was absolutely disgusting and heart-wrenching, but now isn't the time for us to relive it. We need to take care of ourselves and be prepared for our time as rat accordions," he said, looking at Goe, hoping he would laugh like I had.

"Are you serious right now, Rud? Are you really telling jokes? " Goe replied in disgust, looking at me for some help.

"Yes, Goe. Yes, I am. If we're going to make it through this shit, we need to stay the rats we were before this, or at least some semblance of them," Rud replied, giving me his infamous wink.

"Unreal. GW? You seriously onboard with this wackjob?" Goe asked.

"Sorry, Goe, but he's right, you know. If we don't try and keep our sanity, we'll end up like the rats from last night," I replied with a shrug.

Goe wasn't impressed; he just huffed and turned his back on us.

The box started to open, and as the light began to stream in, Rud kept the lightheartedness coming. "It's musical lungs time! Let's get our accordion on! See you on the other side, GW."

We fist-bumped and waited for Bob to set us up.

Being okay with having a foreign green substance injected into me just to experience things was kind of sickening, but at the same time, being in a prison makes you lose any sense of what you're fighting for. I knew it wasn't right, but nothing about our time here had been right.

When it was finally my turn, I closed my eyes and felt the cursed feeling of it coursing through my veins. I didn't open my eyes again until I felt the pressure in my extremities and saw the flash of light through my eyelids.

I began clenching my fists in anticipation and bringing them up to my face, and once the human form returned, I began to shadowbox in excitement. My hands were so large it felt like I was creating wind with every punch. The power these beings must have been even more immense than I could have imagined.

Now, if only I could figure out how they had been able to control the moon.

Not wanting to waste time, I ran over to the pond, picked up the first rock I could find, and hurled it as far as I could. The distance was incredible, and as I watched the rock splash down, images of BJ shot into my brain. If I was able to throw a rock that far, BJ must have…

I couldn't say it out loud, but I felt a shiver go up my spine and a tear fall down my cheek, knowing how hard he must have hit that door. "FUCK," I said, taking everything in me to shake the memory from my brain.

I reminded myself that I would be pulled out of this reality soon and needed to get the most out of it I could. *What else is around here? Where are those flowers that are making this beautiful scent?*

Looking around, I was able to spot a small patch of pearl-white flowers that were so much more beautiful than the giant dandelions we had back in town. However, grabbing one by the stem just under its petals caused me to snatch my hand back in pain. I had grabbed a thorn that tore open one of my fingers. The blood was thick and deep red, just like my rat blood. Licking it confirmed that it tasted just the same as well.

Is this my real blood, or is this what human blood is? Are they the same on the inside as us? Are we just tiny fur-covered humans? No, that would be impossible. We're

rats, and they're humans, but clearly, we must have similarities. The question is, how similar are we? Inspecting
the wound had me wondering. *When I wake up, will my
real hand be cut as well? Am I bleeding into the casket
right now?*

So many questions flew at me as if they were coming
from every direction. How naïve I had been to think
coming back to this human form would bring me more
clarity and understanding of what humans were like.
All it had done was bring on more questions. Hopefully,
Rud was having a better go at it than me.

As time stretched on and I had still did not wake
up, I started to wonder what was wrong. *Shouldn't I be
awake by now? Man, am I going to go insane with all
these unanswered questions? This is getting a little ridiculous at this point.*

"Wake me up, wake me up, wake me up!" I started to
chant. Over and over again, I chanted the same thing,
until finally, the pain shot through my temples and the
world went black. The pinpricks relieved the pressure in
my limbs, and I was able to lift my head just enough to
look down at my hand.

No blood, and no cut! Amazing, I thought. *That means nothing I do in there has any consequence out here. That also means their blood is just like ours. From the color to the taste, we have the same blood coursing through our bodies. That wasn't what I expected to learn today.*

Bob put me back into a box, I started sweating almost immediately, as, to my surprise, there was no one else there with me. Trying to not let my brain go hurtling into a dark place wasn't easy. Luckily for me, the walk back to the prison wasn't long, because I was starting to have a hard time breathing.

Upon arriving back to the cell, my deepest fears were put to rest for the moment, as Rud was there waiting for me with a grin on his face. "You thought I didn't make it, didn't you? Don't lie," he said as his shit-eating grin grew larger.

"Didn't you think it was odd I wasn't there when you got back? I was scared shitless, you know that, and I'm not ashamed to admit it!" I shot back.

"Nah, I could hear the humans discussing the time difference between the different caskets, and I knew you would be coming back a little later than me. Something about them monitoring the difference in effects based on time, fuck if I know what the differences could be but I was only in there for a tiny bit longer than last time. All I did was run! Ran faster than I've ever ran in my life! It was beyond liberating after being trapped in here for so long," he exclaimed.

"You put those longer legs to use, did you? I'm surprised you knew how to use them. I didn't have as much fun as you, but I did reaffirm something about these humans: they bleed just like us, and have the same blood coursing through their veins as we do. I knew I tasted blood when I bit it but more importantly, anything that happens in there does not translate to your body out here. Cutting my hand open on a thorn was quite the experience, I tell you," I replied with a bit too much enthusiasm, which caused a good ribbing from him.

"What are you, a masochist? What, did you purposely cut yourself to retaste the blood of your enemy?" he said with a hearty laugh.

Looking over at him, I showed my teeth and hissed as if I were a bat, which sent us both into hysterical laughter. It felt so good to be able to laugh, and it was doing a great job distracting us from all the craziness we were experiencing.

Right up until we saw her, and everything came crashing down around us once more.

In walked the Mother of Death holding Bissy in one hand and our daily food rations in the other. I looked back over at Rud, whose smile disappeared and been replaced with despair.

Bissy didn't look well at all. She looked as if she was barely breathing, and her eyes were closed, as if she were still under the influence of the serum. She had square patches of missing fur on her back that each looked like they had round scabs in the middle of them, and her skin looked almost grey instead of the pink hue it normally had.

Jenny had started to open the cage beside us when she saw us pressed up against the glass, staring at Bissy. It almost looked like she had a look of remorse and compassion on her face as she started to speak. "Hey, little guys, did you miss her? I guess it can't hurt if I put her back in with you guys for the night. You take care of her, alright? She's still a little groggy, but she'll be okay."

Really? Compassion? I couldn't believe it. *The heartless mother of death may actually have a heart?*

Rud picked Bissy up and carried her into the shack. She still hadn't opened her eyes, but upon her head hitting his chest, a small smile started to form on her face. He set her down on his bed, sniffling, and I figured I would go and collect some water and food to bring inside for them. I wasn't going to get in the way of the two lovebirds' reunion. My heart was swelling with happiness for them, and it, along with seeing the woman whom I had grown to loathe show some compassion towards us had me wondering if there was still some hope left for us after all.

I took two steps into the door, staring at the water bowl, trying to make sure I didn't spill it, and instantly had to turn around the moment I looked up and saw that Bissy's eyes were open and staring deeply into Rud's as their lips met. They didn't notice me, as they were fixated on each other, but even so, I felt bad, as if I had walked in on a special moment meant just for them.

Sitting down outside the door, I took out a carrot and began to chomp away quietly. Staring out over the less than half-full wall adjacent to us, my mind started to drift towards what would have happened if we hadn't been captured. Would Rud have found sobriety? Would Bissy have met and fallen in love with him, as she had along this dreadful journey? If anything, at least they each had some positive change come from this.

But what about me?

Before I could go too far down the rabbit hole of despair, I felt a hand on my shoulder. Looking up, I met Bissy's eyes. They were bloodshot red, just like mine, but I could see happiness beaming out of them as if the kiss had sparked an extra glimmer.

"GW, I hope you know that I care for you as well. Not the way I do Rud, but you've become family to me. If it weren't for you, Rud and I never would have met, let alone made it this far. Thank you from the bottom of my heart for being you, and even more so for giving us space earlier," she said with a wink as she leaned down and kissed me on the cheek.

I could've sworn my white fur went completely red from embarrassment. "I didn't think you guys noticed me. Thank you for that, Bissy. You've become the sister I never had, and Rud has become the big brother I always wanted," I replied.

"Big brother, eh? I don't know, man; you act well older than me," Rud interrupted as he stepped out of the doorway, ending with his infectious laugh.

We all broke into laughter, and after Bissy helped me up, we all joined in a long family-like hug. I couldn't help but start to cry. The emotion of realizing I still had them as a family of sorts sent tears flying. They were my second family!

Chapter 7

T he next few days were uneventful in terms of experiments, and we were left to ourselves as we waited our turn, watching as small groups of five rats came and went. We assumed that this was because there weren't many of us left.

As the days passed, the time Bissy and Rud spent alone together in the shack got longer and longer, and I could only assume what they were doing in there. There was no way I was going to go and verify my thoughts, though, as the nights already had me wishing I had some earplugs. Don't take this the wrong way, but hearing your friends consummate their love for each other is also a kind of torture—maybe not at the same level of these hellish experiments, but torture nonetheless.

By Day Four, I was dying for my turn to get back in the rat accordion to human machine. By this point, Rud only came out of the shack to get food and bring it back inside, giving me a dirty wink every time he did. It was hilarious and gross all at the same time.

How much fornication can one couple do every day? We're supposed to be rats, not rabbits, I ruminated.

It wasn't until Day Five that my wishes were granted, but I regretted it immediately. Both Jenny and Bob came into the room in what seemed to be in a panicked state. They always walked in so calmly and went about their business, but today, something was off. Each of them had two boxes in their hands, and they started loading all the rats, including the ones they had used the past few days.

It was definitely odd, and even their conversations with each other were off. Jenny wasn't barking orders at Bob. It seemed like he was the one leading the conversations for once. "Jenny, we've got this, okay? I know they've bumped our timeline up again, but you and I both know this is for the betterment of our race. We've led this research for over a year now, and are light years ahead of anyone else," Bob said after filling the first box.

"I know, I know, but there's still so much work left to be done. Our DNA-altering experiments are not even close to being done. The cats are almost there, but the dogs and pigeons are a ways off, not to mention the tests on that female rat," she replied with a frantic undertone in her voice.

"Yes, we know the muscle growth is working but we can continue that off-planet during our cryo-sleep if we get these linked trials complete in the coming days. We seem to have figured out the BA-1 with AR-2, so now, it's just the links and food distribution we need to get ironed out before we move on to humans," he replied with a calm demeanor that I had never seen in him before.

"Alright, so are you wanting to move to adding the food or doing the linked AR experience today? We only have two days left after today," Jenny asked.

"Let's do the AR link today, and we'll start on the food this afternoon or tomorrow at the latest. The AR link should be fairly simple, so let's bang that out. If you want to check on the female rat's progression, we can do that after," Bob replied as he continued to box up the last of the rats from the other side of the room.

Jenny moved over to our side and started going through the lower shelves, so I figured I'd better go let Rud know their time is up. It would be a matter of minutes before she took us out of here.

Running back into the shack, I saw that the two of them were dead asleep, with Bissy snuggled right into Rud's arms. It wasn't the wakeup call I wanted to give them, but it had to be done.

Walking over to Rud's side of the bed, I lightly shook him until I could see his eyes starting to move behind his eye lids. "Rud, you got to wake up, man. They're here to take us for another go in the human machine," I whispered.

He opened one eye sheepishly and turned to look at me. "Huh?" he replied.

"Jenny is here, and they're taking us all for another round of tests. Any second now. You got to get up."

Both of his eyes shot open when his groggy brain realized what I was saying. "You got to be kidding. I just got to sleep. Help me slide out of here so we don't wake Bissy up," he replied with a hint of anger and disappointment in his voice.

Before I could help him, the shack was pulled back, and as I looked up, I could see Jenny's expression change. It started with confusion, then went to anger, then right onto looking like a lightbulb had lit up. She put the shack back down and called for Bob. "Bob, you won't believe this, but I think our DNA rat test just got an exciting twist. The female has a mate!" she said with an excitement I hadn't heard come from her mouth before.

"Well, then, that's a twist. That is for sure. We'll need him for this link test, but we can isolate the two of them afterwards, will be really interesting to see how their offspring are effected." Bob replied with a small chuckle.

What did he mean, "isolate the two of them?" No fucking way. I just got my second family back together a few days ago. There's no way I can let them split us up again. If I have to go through the rest of this without them, I don't think I can make it.

The shack came back off again, and Jenny grabbed Rud and me. Bissy had woken up, and was trying with all her might to hold Rud's hand as she tried to outmuscle the mother of death. It was a short-lived battle, but as Bissy's grip slipped and Jenny started to lift Rud out of the cage, he turned to give her some assurance. "It will be okay; I'll be back shortly, and we can chat about those names we were discussing."

"Names?" I was completely confused, but didn't think much of it, as Bissy had started to bawl, and Jenny was already lifting me out.

"Is she going to be alright, man?" I asked as soon as Jenny put me down in the box beside Rud.

"She's a tough one; she'll be fine. You saw the marks on her, and she has to deal with me, so I'd say she's been through worse," Rud replied with his token wink at the end.

I couldn't help but laugh at that one, and then I gave him one of his famous lines right back. "You ready for accordion time?"

"Time to do some huffing and puffing. I need a good run, anyways," he replied as we could feel the box being set back down.

They started taking us out two by two, and both Rud and I realized it at the same time. We gave each other a fist bump and put an arm around each other so they would be forced to pick us together. Our ploy worked, as Bob reached in and grabbed the two of us.

"Ah, look who it is. It's the lover boy and the shit disturber," Bob said as he looked down at us in his hands. Neither of us even attempted to respond, as we knew he wouldn't understand us anyways.

We could see rows of caskets sitting two by two instead of the regular singular rows, one right behind the other, with what looked to be one breathing tube with two masks hanging above them. I was so distracted looking down at them that I didn't notice Jenny walking over with the needles until I felt the sting on the back of my neck.

The numbing feeling of the BA-1 taking over my body was still incredibly off-putting. It caused the craziest nausea I had ever felt, and my body couldn't deal with it by vomiting, since my bodily functions were subdued.

The order of things didn't change, with the breathing machine coming next, then the goggles, then the pressure returning to my extremities, which I had come to realize was the AR serum being injected through many small needles lining my entire body. It had become a comforting part of the process, as it killed the nausea almost immediately. The pressure also signaled that I needed to close my eyes to avoid the blinding white light from the goggles.

Hearing the casket close was the last step before we knew the human experience would start again.

I had been expecting to open my eyes to lush green grass, the smell of wildflowers, and the pond in the distance, but to my surprise, I woke up in the middle of a forest. It must have been Fall, as all the leaves were all different hues of red, orange, and yellow. The breeze was strong, causing a few leaves to blow free from their branches. The sight of them falling to the forest floor was mesmerizing. I had never been allowed up and over the falls back home after summer, and so I'd only caught a glimpse of the trees changing from afar. Even then, they had been a sight to behold. The sound of the leaves falling in the wind, the many shades of colors, and the leaves crunching under my feet was a breathtaking experience.

"GW?" a male voice echoed in the distance.

"Rud? Is that you? Where you at, bro?"

It sounded like he was in front of me, but I couldn't see him through the trees and thick undergrowth. I found myself squinting to try and see any motion, but the falling leaves made it hard to focus.

A snap from a breaking tree branch startled me as it caught me off-guard, coming from behind me. I whipped my head around, and yet I found nothing.

"GW?" the male voice returned with a louder echo this time. It sounded as if it was coming from behind the thick brush to my right.

I started to walk cautiously towards the bushes and replied to the voice again. "Rud? Come on man!"

Leaning towards the bush, I reached out to pull the leaves aside so I could try and see through it.

"GAHHH!" I screamed as something grabbed my foot, sending me ass over tea kettle into a pile of leaves behind me.

Rud came out from under the bush, laughing hysterically and pointing at me. "Bro, you should see your scared human face! Ha, ha, ha. It's even funnier than your scared rat face. Here, come on. Get your ass out of those leaves." He reached out to help me up, but I was furious, so I grabbed his hand and pulled him down into the leaves. He was still laughing as I threw a few punches into his belly, causing his chuckles to turn to coughs. "Calm down, lil' man! Geez, I don't have a cushy rat belly, and that kind of hurts," he choked out.

"Good, I hope it hurts. You almost made me shit myself there!" I replied as my reactionary anger started to subside and the humor of the situation took hold.

"Alright, alright!" he said, still chuckling. "This forest is sweet, eh? The leaves are next-level. Let's go for a little hike and see what we can find."

We started to head west. It looked like it was uphill, and we were hoping to get a view. At first, there was no trail, and the going was slow as we ducked and weaved under branches and through thick undergrowth. After about thirty minutes of hard going, though, we came across a cutout that was absent of trees and filled with low-cut brown grass. It was a perfectly square clearing, which you would never see in nature, and it was a little off-putting, but what's natural in this fake world?

Before we sat down, Rud asked me what I thought the name of this place was, but instead of answering his question, all I could think of was one of the last things he'd said to Bissy: "We can chat about those names we were discussing."

"Speaking of names, what were you and Bissy talking about?"

"You caught that, eh? You been thinking about that this whole time?" Rud replied with a devilish grin on his face.

"Literally just thought about it now when you asked me about this place. And, to answer your question, I have no damn idea."

"Well, GW, let me put it this way: it's looking like you may be an uncle," Rud proclaimed with his grin growing into a full-blown clown smile it was so big.

"No fucking way! Are you serious? How could you even know?" I said while my brain tried to decide if it was more shocked or excited.

"Bissy says she knows. She said she started to feel different the other day and just knew," he said before pausing and looking up at the clouds overhead. "We know the chances are slim but if we ever get out of here, we want you to be the godfather. We want you to be what BJ was to your father."

"Don't talk like that, we are going to get out of here alive and is that even a question? I'll be the greatest uncle this world has ever seen. But 'him?' Like you know it's going to be a boy?"

"Nah, just hoping," he said with a Rud-wink.

"I don't even know what to say right now. I'm beyond excited for you two, and will do everything I can to make sure we all get out of here," I replied, putting my hand on his shoulder. "You're going to make a great father, Rud. No need to go back to the bottle now, eh?"

He looked at me, and for a brief second, I thought he was going to punch me, but then he looked back up to the clouds and laughed. "You're right, GW. The only bottle I'll be going back to is to fill the baby's bottle with milk."

We sat there in silence for a few moments, just staring up at the clouds as they slowly rolled by, before Rud jumped up. "Do you see that trail over there on the west side of the cut?" he said, pointing over to a break in the trees. Squinting, I was able to see the break in the trees, but I couldn't quite make out a trail. "I'll race ya! Maybe you can actually keep up with me with those giant legs you've got now?" he said, doing an odd body movement that looked as if he were trying to stretch.

"You're on! You do the countdown—3,2,1, baby— and we start on baby!" I replied as I tried to mimic his stretch.

"On baby, eh?" he said with a chuckle. "Alright. 3...2...1... BABY!"

We both bolted for the opening. For the first ten feet or so, I had the jump on him, but as we got to about the halfway point, I looked back, and had he started to close the gap. Before we were three-quarters of the way, he'd passed me and stretched his lead a good three to four strides. He looked back at me, and as we locked eyes, he disappeared for a moment before reappearing as if he hadn't missed a stride. He kept doing it all the way to the clearing. He was blinking on and off like the lights in the casket.

"You alright, man? I think something is up with the...what did the humans call it? Your link?" I said to him as I tried to catch my breath.

"Yeah, I'm all good, but I kept jumping back and forth between the casket and here. It was incredibly hard to stay focused, but I wasn't going to let anything stop me from handing you a hefty loss," he replied, breathing as if he hadn't even run, let alone run at full-tilt for the entire way.

It amazed me that our physical fitness level and acumen transferred over to this alternate reality, but what happened here physically didn't translate back. The memories certainly did, which had my brain all sorts of confused. Being here as a human was already a giant mindfuck, but this just added a whole new level of complexity that I couldn't seem to grasp.

"Told you there was a trail over here. Let's see where this takes us. It looks like it continues uphill," Rud said, interrupting me from my confused state of contemplation.

Rud rounding the corner , stopped abruptly. "Wow!"

As I rounded the corner, my eyes were met with the most beautiful sight I had ever come across. We were standing on top of treelined ridge that overlooked a giant forest below. The trees were all the same hues of orange, red, and yellow, but seeing them from this high above was stunning. There was a stream running through the middle, and as you followed the stream out of the forest, it led you up a towering mountain with snow-covered caps that stretched all the way into the clouds. It reminded me of the pictures in a storybook about mountain cats that my father used to read me.

We had hoped for a view, but this was even better than we could have imagined. If it weren't fake, I would have said this was the most beautiful place on earth.

"If only Bissy could see this," Rud said with a tiny sniffle.

"I know, man. I know. I'm not half as pretty, and I definitely won't be kissing you, no matter how pretty the view is," I replied, trying to lighten his mood and help bring him back to the present.

"'Half as pretty?' You're funnier than me sometimes, GW. Have you seen your red eyes? You're *horrifying*," he said trading his sniffles for laughter.

We sat there for what felt like an hour or two, taking in the beauty and trading barbs back and forth, until the AR serum wore off and we were transported back to reality. It felt great to experience it and have some time with my brother, as it wouldn't be long before we would be back in our glass cage, where I would lose him to Bissy, shacking up for hours in their room. Rud had pulled a bunch of the wood chips into the shack to create their own little room inside. He said it was so I could have some privacy, but we both knew it was so they could have their own space. It had hurt at first when he'd done it, but after hearing their news, I was kind of happy they had .

When we got back into the transport box, I was happy to see Goe was there. It had been probably a week since our last meeting, and I hoped he wasn't still upset with us for joking with him. He looked fairly gaunt. His face was significantly thinner, and his brown fur had started to get quite a few greys in it.

"Goe, you still upset with us, man?" Rud said as he looked at me with a smirk. Goe didn't even acknowledge him. I thought he may have been still angry, but on second glance, I saw that his facial expression never changed, and he didn't even flinch a muscle.

I walked over to him, and he didn't even seem to see me. "Goe!" I said loudly right in front of him. His eyes didn't move, but I saw his ears twitch.

"GW, is that you?" Goe replied as he gazed right through me.

"Yeah, Goe. I'm right here in front of you."

"My eyes have failed me, and I can barely hear anymore. I'm not sure if it was these stupid experiments, or if my age has finally caught up with me. Pretty sure it's a combination of both," he said with a hint of depression in his voice.

"Yeah, man, I think it may be a bit of both, as even your coat has quite a bit of grey in it," I replied as Rud walked over to us.

"Goe, it's all that pent-up stress, man. Told you, you need to laugh more and take it easy," Rud chimed in.

"Rud, dude, come on, man. Take it easy on the poor old guy," I murmured.

"I may be old, but I'm not too old to have a sense of humor, or to fight my own battles, for that matter. It's all good. He's right, you know. This place has really sent me spiraling. Teeth grinding every night and a severe lack of appetite is starting to take its toll. But, GW, if you call me a 'poor old guy' again, I'll find you in this darkness and smack the shit out of you," Goe responded before breaking out into a chuckle.

We all had a hearty laugh as the transport box got picked up, and it continued through the entire bumpy journey back to our prison. By the time we got back and the box started to open, my face and belly were aching from all the laughing.

There was a big meal waiting for us upon our return, and Bissy made sure that all three of us sat down together to enjoy it. She'd pushed up some wood chips up against the glass so we could sit and look out over the room. It was no forest-and-mountain view, but it was all we had in this reality.

Rud did his best to explain the view to her, but the main part of his story revolved around him destroying me in the race. He certainly loved his speedy prowess.

We could see poor Goe eating alone on the other side of the room. I hadn't realized when we were talking earlier that all his cagemates had passed during the experiments. It made a lot more sense as to why he was taking it so hard. If I didn't have Rud and Bissy, I'd imagine I wouldn't be taking it with humor, either. At least my fur was all white, so you wouldn't notice the greys, though.

After dinner, Rud and Bissy went off to their room, but I decided to sit out for a little while so I could try to enjoy the quiet. All the remaining rats had already gone in for the night, even though the lights were still on. Only Goe was still out, sitting with his eyes closed and breathing deeply. It looked as if he was meditating. The poor old guy must be lonely over there; there weren't many rats left on his side of the room. Even the cages to either side of him were empty. It was sad, but before heading in for the night, I couldn't help but watch him until Jenny came to turn off the lights.

It had felt like an extra-long day, and I was so beat that as soon as my head hit the bed, I was out like a light. I woke up with a smile on my face and a pep in my step, as the previous day had been great all around.

But that only lasted until I finished breakfast. Rud and Bissy were still in their room when Bob and Jenny came into the room carrying one small box and two of the red needles they'd used on Bissy. My brain instantly brought back Bob's words from the day before—"We can isolate the two of them after."

Panic set in, and I raced back into the shack.

"What's wrong, GW? You look like you've seen a ghost," Rud said the moment I came crashing through the door.

"They're here for you and Bissy! They know what you two have been doing, and they want to isolate you! I can't let them take you. I can't!"

Before he could respond, the top of the cage came off, and Bob removed the shack. I crouched down beside Rud, waiting to attack, but instead of going for Rud, he went for Bissy first, scooping her up before Rud or I could react. We watched as he stuck her sleeping body with the needle and put her into the box.

Rud looked at me and pleaded for me to let him go without putting up a fight so that he could be with Bissy. "Just let me go, man. I can't let her go alone. Hopefully, we'll be back soon."

"I can't...I can't be alone!" I cried.

Bob cautiously started for Rud, but instead of waiting, Rud jumped right into his hand. I leapt behind him and caught Bob's pinky finger with my nails. They punctured the skin and gave me enough grip to pull my head up and bite down, causing Bob to jerk his hand back, sending both Rud and I tumbling back into the wood chips.

"You little shit! I told you you were going to pay, and now I damn well mean it! You'll regret this one day soon." Bob yelled.

As I got back to my feet, I could see Rud coming towards me, absolutely fuming. "I told you to let me go man! Fuck!" He shoved me back to the ground and put his foot on my chest. "I love you, brother, but stay the fuck down. I need to be with her and my unborn child. We'll be back for you, I promise!"

Tears started to fall down my cheeks as I watched Bob encase Rud in his other hand and stick him with the second needle before loading him into the box with Bissy.

As they walked out the door and it closed behind them, I saw Goe sitting there watching. My heart dropped even further.

Now, just like him, I was alone.

Chapter 8

My eyes didn't leave the door all day. I only allowed them to blink when they started to feel like dried-out raisins. These humans had taken everything and everyone I had ever loved. The only reason I had to keep going was the small chance that Rud and Bissy might actually return. *What else is there at this point?*

The door handle started to turn, causing me to jump to my feet. *Please be them*, I prayed, but as Bob came into the room, I knew they weren't with him. He was carrying the large transport box, not the little one they had left in.

The experiments would continue, and I would have to face them alone.

Bob loaded the other wall of rats first before moving over to my side of the room. I must have gotten him good, because I could see the blood pooling around the white bandage on his finger. He left me until last and put on a pair of gloves before reaching in for me. He didn't need them, though, as I didn't have any energy left to fight him. I was feeling too sorry for myself to care.

Goe was sitting in the corner across from me, his nose twitching as he smelled the air. "GW, come over here," he called out. "I know you're in here. I can smell your poor young ass."

I wanted to wallow in my sorrow by myself, but I couldn't ignore him. I got up, went over, and sat down beside him.

"You aren't one to keep quiet, GW. What happened last night? I could hear Rud yelling and that human getting angry," Goe said.

I didn't want to answer, but I also wanted to get it off my chest. "They took Rud and Bissy away from me. They took them and left me alone! I have no idea where they went, but the humans said that they were isolating them. I'm all alone, Goe, just like you, and Rud even wanted to leave me."

"Did Rud want to leave you, or did he not want to be separated from Bissy? A rat's love is undying; you shouldn't take it as a slight towards you. I disowned my own mother and father for my wife, God rest her soul," Goe replied.

Deep down, I knew he was right. Rud didn't want to leave me, but it still hurt, and if they didn't return, I didn't know if I'd be able to forgive myself for letting them go.

We sat in silence for the remainder of the short trip to the experiment room. When we arrived, it was Jenny who opened the box, not Bob, and she still looked panicked and worn out. The scratches on her face from BJ had healed, but they had been replaced by big dark spots under her eyes.

We locked eyes, and it felt as if my sorrow could read hers. Something was definitely bothering her, but there was no way for me to communicate with her to figure it out. Her expression almost made me feel bad for her, but I couldn't. She was a part of the reason I felt my own sorrow.

Something was different today. As she held me, I could see the line of caskets were back in singular rows, and there was another tube hanging beside each air mask. Once Jenny stuck me with the BA-1 serum and my body went limp, I expected her to grab the air mask, but instead, she laid me down, held my mouth open with one hand, and started to slide the other tube into my mouth and then down my throat. The sensation was excruciating, and only made the normal nausea that much worse. I could feel the tube hit my stomach before she stopped pushing it in and put the air mask over my face.

The AR needles couldn't come soon enough to kill the nausea, but to my chagrin, it didn't help with the discomfort of the tube in my belly. I wanted nothing more than to rip the tube out of my mouth, but the BA serum made that impossible.

As the goggles powered up, I felt a tiny bit of relief, as the visual stimulation was a welcome distraction. This time, instead of being transported into nature, it looked like a bright bedroom. I was lying in a bed that was so plush and warm that I didn't want to get out. It certainly wasn't the straw or woodchip beds I was used to.

Looking around the room, I could see a wall of books, a desk, and a fresh set of clothes at the foot of the bed. As I contemplated how long I could stay in this cloudlike bed, my nose caught a whiff of some mouthwatering food coming from beyond the bedroom door. My stomach growled as if it hadn't eaten breakfast a few hours ago.

Once the hunger became unbearable, making staying in bed almost impossible, I begrudgingly got up and got dressed. As I slowly headed out the door and down the stairs, the smell grew stronger and stronger with every step. Rounding the corner at the bottom of the stairs, I was met by a meal meant for royalty: a giant cheese plate with every type imaginable, steamed vegetables, and a warm basket of freshly cooked buns that reminded me of the ones Goe used to serve at his bakery while you waited in line for your order.

When I started to eat, I could hear an odd pumping noise in the distance that stopped every time I stopped eating. It was incredibly off-putting, so I pushed my plate a side and went for the front door with one last piece of cheese in my hand.

I took a bite as I stepped outside. Everything went black, and I shot back to reality.

As the goggles went clear, returning me to reality, I could hear the pumping noise becoming louder. I watched as a yellow liquid was pumped down the tube in front of me, into my mouth, and then into my stomach.

Being force-fed as I ate in an alternate reality was so far beyond my brain's computing power that it must have caused me to pass out. When I came to, the top of my casket was off, the tube was out of my throat, and only the air mask was still attached. Even the AR needles had been released, and, to my surprise, I was able to move my arms.

My legs were still asleep, but I sat up and looked down the row of caskets. Bob and Jenny were both a few caskets down from me, unplugging the machine. It looked as if they were trying to break into the thing.

They were trying to pry it open when there was a loud sound almost like a balloon popping. It echoed through the room, causing them to drop the casket on the table. A gross mixture of red and yellow began to ooze from the casket before the lid popped open, revealing a sight so grotesque both Bob and Jenny vomited onto the floor. If I weren't still under the effects of the BA-1 serum, I would have done the same.

It was as if the rat inside had exploded from the neck down to its thighs. Its face was unrecognizable; it was covered in a mixture of bloody ooze, and the lower portion of its jaw was missing.

"My god, that's vile! Did you not load the AR food mechanics to this one? How the hell did the feeding machine malfunction to the point of making this rat explode!?" Jenny cried as she wiped chunks of vomit from her chin.

"It had the same AR food amount programmed as all of the rest. This has to be a software or hardware malfunction. We'll have to dissect this from a data point, pull the memory card, and send it and the machine down to engineering. Don't clean the machine, either, so they can see what we have to deal with when they fuck up. We definitely can't go to stage 2 with this kind of catastrophic error. We're running out of time and rats, dammit," Bob asserted.

"I don't think I can stomach taking this down there like this. The smell is horrific, let alone the sight of this poor guy," Jenny said. She put her hand back to her mouth to stop herself from losing even more of her stomach's contents.

"Fine. I'll take it. Pass me the memory bank, and I'll meet you down there so we can go over the data points with them. We need to figure this out ASAP and get back to it first thing in the morning. Another sleepless night. Fucking wonderful," Bob replied before heading out the door.

My heart and mind were racing as I quickly laid back down so he wouldn't spot me as he left. The blood, the gore, the disfigured face and body—it was all too much, and I couldn't get the images out of my brain.

Luckily, it wasn't long before Jenny came to take my breathing mask off and put me back into the transport box. I could see her crying the whole time, and I wondered why I was feeling so sorry for her again. *Am I mad for having empathy for the Mother of Death?*

She is holding Bissy and Rud hostage, and has taken all of your family and friends from you, I reminded myself. *Still, is she doing this against her will? She clearly isn't enjoying this!*

My mind was a confused mess of a puzzle, fighting itself about feeling anything but anger towards this human. When I finally found a moment to gather myself and look around the box, my feelings towards her shot right back to anger. *Goe! Where is he!?*

"Goe!" I yelled, pushing through everyone as I searched for him. "Goe! Goe!"

Everyone else was here.

Don't tell me it was Goe, of all the rats! He was the rat that was fed to death? How the fuck could I have been so stupid as to feel sorry for the witch, the mother of death?!

I can only imagine the torture Goe must have gone through as he was force-fed over and over to the point of his skin no longer being able to contain his internal organs.

How is this even possible? Every single person I have known or ever loved is gone!

It wasn't like Goe was family or anything, but he was the last rat I knew who was still alive. A few I could say were a coincidence, but every single person? I had to be cursed and this curse had taken them all.

It was another long and sleepless night, as I couldn't get the grotesque scene out of my mind. It was absolutely sickening and horrific. Every time I closed my eyes, I could see Goe's jawless face staring at me, haunting me. It was baked right into the back of my eyelids.

The next morning couldn't come soon enough, and I honestly hoped it would be my last on this Earth. Hearing Bob and Jenny talking as they came down the hall gave me hope that I might get my wish. I knew Bob had it in for me this whole time. He had warned me he would make me pay for biting him so many times.

"Alright, so—this is the start of our final test before we move to human trials. Let's finish this out strong.

Luckily, that mishap yesterday was a mechanical malfunction, 'cause if it was code-based, that could have finished us," Bob said as he opened the door.

"At this point, will we even have time for human trials? I heard the Europeans are moving towards launch of their first wave in two weeks," Jenny replied as she put on her gloves and buttoned up her long white coat.

"I was talking to my friend who works on their team over there, and he can't believe they're launching. They skipped the feeding trials on rats and moved straight to human testing. It's a shitshow over there, and he thinks the Asian peninsula is even further behind," Bob said as he prepared the transport box and lined up the BA-1 needles on the desk.

"Yeah, it seems we have the best system so far. My girlfriend in China and I were on a VR chat last night, and she was asking me how we solved the nausea symptoms using the AR serum. Their version seems to be making it worse. She showed me the sequencing, and it looks fairly similar to ours, but something is up with the proteins they're using. They looked almost completely synthetic," Jenny continued.

"You better not have shown them our sequencing! The lab has a digital track on all files! You know the penalties," Bob snapped, turning to see Jenny's reaction.

"Do I have *Stupid* written across my forehead? I'm not risking my family's ticket off this rock, let alone my own!" Jenny quipped as she grabbed the rat below me out of their cage.

"You know I had to ask," Bob replied as Jenny started to lift the lid on my cage.

"Leave that little shit white rat for me. I have something special lined up for him today," he said as he put his bite-proof gloves on and started towards me. "Told you I would make you pay, you little shit!" he said to me with hate in his eyes.

"Are you seriously holding a grudge against a rat?" Jenny interjected.

"Say what you want. Yes. Yes, I am. This little shit has been nothing but trouble since the first day we met!" Bob replied as Jenny started to snicker.

I welcomed his grasp, and hoped that his so-called revenge would soon send me to see my family in the afterlife. There was nothing left for me in this world.

Instead, I got something much worse.

There were only ten or fifteen of us left in the transport box, and we all sat silently. The others must have felt fairly similar to me, as not a single one looked at another. I could see the exhaustion and lack of appetite for life in their faces, and I was sure the look on my own was very much the same.

We arrived in the cold and scentless room, and I could see the caskets lined up, but this time there was a marker on each one—*1 week, 2 weeks, 3 weeks*, and on and on until I got to the one at the end, which had nothing but numbers on it and a warning.

It read *2050—Do Not Open.*

That one must be for me, I thought.

Bob and Jenny began to load the other rats into their caskets, and just before they got to me, Jenny looked at Bob. "2050!? Bob, are you serious right now?" she asked with a look of confusion.

"I told you I had something planned for him. Trust me, this was incredibly cathartic for me to plan," he replied.

"Twenty-three years!? They want us to be gone within the year. You can't be serious," she said.

"I'm serious, this little guy is going to wake up in a whole different world. Don't worry; I have the pod hooked up to the solar battery backup for the building, and I loaded the food dispenser with more than enough food. I even hooked up a DNA-1 drip," Bob said with a grin.

"The only thing I can't do is be here to see this little shit's reaction when he wakes up and the world is empty," he replied before erupting into laughter.

"You're insane. How long did you spend preparing this? You seriously went through all this just to get back at a little rat?" Jenny replied, going into her own evil chuckle.

"Long enough, but Donnie in engineering did the coding of the machine, so not as much as you would think. He even loaded his new cryo-learning software, so if this works, he'll awaken with enough knowledge to know how fucked he is," Bob said, continuing to laugh uncontrollably.

All the other rats were loaded at this point, and all that was left sitting there waiting for me was my casket, which was quite a bit bigger than the others. There was no way I could survive as long as Bob planned, so all I could hope was that I died sooner rather than later. I had known he was going to get back at me, but this wasn't what I'd expected. A quick death after the trials were over was what I had hoped for. This wasn't that. This was a long and torturous death.

I tried to fight Bob when he came for me, but the gloves were too thick, and instead of trying to pick me up, he just pinned me down and stuck me with the BA-1 serum, sending my body into paralysis instantly.

When my casket shut, my thoughts instantly went to Bissy and Rud. Hopefully, they didn't have to endure a similar fate, and would make it out of here with their little one in tow. Bob had never carried a grudge against them like he did me, so I had a glimmer of hope that the curse might just end with my death, and I hoped it would happen sooner rather than later. Twenty-three years is a long damn time.

I awoke in the same cushy bed as the last trial, with the same wall of books and the same fresh clothes at the foot of the bed. The only difference this time was that there was no smell calling me to get up.

Rolling onto my side and curling up, I noticed a book called *Cryo Guide to Sleep Learning* and what seemed to be a clock on the night table. It wasn't in hours, days, or even months, though; it just showed twenty twenty-seven in bright red.

"Are you kidding me? The clock beside my bed won't change except every three hundred and sixty-five days?" I said in dismay.

Rolling back over, I stared at the wall of books and started counting them in hopes that would lull me back to sleep. Counting things used to work as a kid, but as I scanned, the book titles got more and more interesting. "*Field Medical Skills, Survival Skills 101, Robotics I, II,* and *III, Mammalian Anatomy and Physiology,* and a whole slew of science books!? As interesting as these seem, where are the storybooks that can distract me from this reality?" I said.

After what felt like an hour or two, I had an idea. Not even bothering to put the clothes on, I jumped out of bed and rushed down the stairs and through the kitchen. Then, grabbing the door handle, I whipped the front door open.

I had thought maybe I could wake myself back up by going out the front door, like the last time I was in this place, but as I stepped out the door, I was met by the sun. I dropped to my knees as the weight of being stuck here hit me again. My hopes had been crushed.

I picked myself back up after a good cry, then sulked my way back up the stairs and into the bed. Staring at the white ceiling, I was reminded of an old sleep trick BJ had taught me on one of our camping trips. He used to use it when his sleep schedule would get messed up during his change to night shift at the police station.

"Just fake-close your eyes slowly, as if you were exhausted and falling asleep. Slowly close your eyelids until they touch each other, then force them back open, as if you didn't want to sleep. If you do this long enough, you will trick your body into believing it's tired." I could hear him say it to me as if he were there with me, and after a few minutes of trying, I conked out.

It felt like I slept for days, and what was even more interesting was the dream I had.

When I woke up, I went straight for the book on the side of the bed and opened it up. Reading through the first page I was in shock. I knew every word before I even read it. The *Cryo Guide to Sleep Learning* had been engrained into my memory while I slept, and the meaning behind that was simple, yet incredibly mind-boggling: all I needed to do was grab one of the books each night, put it down on the night table beside the clock, and in the morning, I would awaken with whatever knowledge lay within its pages.

Now I understood what Bob had meant when he said, "He'll wake up with enough knowledge to know how fucked he is."

As I put the book down, my mind was aflutter, but as it hit the table, my nose caught the smell of food, sending my stomach into its own flutter. I grabbed the clothes from the end of the bed, threw them on, unlocked the bedroom door, and headed for the stairs. I stopped at the top, as I heard clanking dishes and what sounded like a chair being pulled out from a table.

"Hello?" I yelled down the stairwell. There was no response.

"Who is there?" I called out again. There was still no response, but I could hear whoever it was get up and walk towards the front door.

"You don't need to run; I'm happy to share the food with you or anything else you may need. Name's GW. I'm going to come down now, and we can introduce ourselves," I said as I started to descend the stairs.

The feeling of relief that I wasn't alone in here far outweighed the fear of who or what could be down there. As I rounded the corner, stopping at the doorway to the kitchen just in case, I looked up and met eyes with a woman. I had forgotten that in this reality, I wasn't a rat, so I was initially shocked to see a female human and not another rat.

"What are you doing here? How did you get in my house?" the lady said with a look of confusion and fear on her face.

"Your house? I thought this was my house. I just woke up from a nap and smelled the food," I replied before hearing the rudeness in my voice and quickly fixing my tone. "Sorry, let's start over here. Name's GW, and yourself?"

"Nikki," she begrudgingly replied.

"Nikki? I don't remember seeing you in the transport box."

"You mean the bus? There were no men on the bus I was on. When did you get here?" Nikki replied.

Bus? What the hell is she talking about? I thought. "I woke up in my bed yesterday, but was very upset, and decided to go back to sleep."

"What? I was down here all day yesterday, and have been here for almost a month, so I would have noticed you come in and go upstairs. Were you in the locked room at the top of the stairs?" Nikki inquired.

I was completely taken aback. *She's been here for a month? Is she mad, or am I?*

As I ran out of the room and back up the stairs, I answered that I had been in the locked room.

As I burst back into my room, I saw the clock and almost fainted.

It read *2028!*

"Are you okay?" Nikki yelled from the bottom of the stairs.

2028! There was no way I slept a whole damn year, was there?

"GW?" Nikki yelled again.

"I'm a bit confused, but I'll be back down in a minute. Sorry," I replied in complete confusion.

If it had been a year since I was here, then that meant Nikki was more than likely not a rat. Bob had said that human trials were supposed to be starting in a few weeks, and if this clock wasn't lying and she had, in fact, been here for a month, it would only make sense.

"Nikki, what year is it?"

"Did you lose your memory when they put you under or something? It's February of 2028. Not sure of the exact day, but I have a calendar in my room," she replied, starting to sound a bit disturbed.

Fuck me. I got to act cool, 'cause there's no way she isn't human at this point, I reminded myself.

"No, no. It's just that my clock only shows the year, which was kind of odd to me, and something felt off. Maybe I'm still a bit groggy from the BA-1 serum."

"BA-1? They gave you the rat stuff!?" she said with a chuckle. "You mean HA-1, right?" Her chuckle turned to full-on laughter.

"Wow, my brain really is foggy," I replied, trying to fake-laugh at my own stupidity.

"It's alright. Come back down here and I'll make you some food. Clear that mind up with a full stomach," she said before heading back into the kitchen and causing a racket, slamming pots and pans around.

She really is a human, and she can actually understand me in this reality, I thought. *Being asleep for a year is crazy, but talking to a human is madness. Being able to understand is one thing, but now, I have to converse with her as if I am one. Not sure how this is going to go, but if I stay up here, she'll definitely think something is really off, and, to be honest, I could use the company.*

"What's that smell!? You cooking up heaven in here?" I said as I came into the kitchen.

"Well, I had some leftover barbeque from last night, so I figured I would warm that up and whip you up a side of spaghetti to go with it. I know they're feeding some godawful protein mixture into our real bodies, but the taste simulation is fantastic," Nikki replied, pulling her hair away from her face as she stirred a boiling bowl of water.

"A side of spaghetti?" I said, perplexed, as my mother would make a similar dish as a whole meal back home.

"I can tell you aren't from the south by the look on your face. You see, to us, spaghetti is a side, and no one will tell me any different," she replied, taking the pot off the stove and walking over to the sink to strain the water.

The way she moved was so graceful compared to Jenny, and the twang in her voice was so soft and soothing, that it made me realize they were nothing alike. If I was going to be here with her, I needed to learn as much from her as I planned to from those books. "Nikki, would it be too upfront of me to ask why you're here? I had heard the rat trials were pretty scary."

"Well, they don't really tell you about the animal trials, but I didn't really have a choice. I don't know how they did it in your town, but in Nashville, it was a lottery. Participants secured first-class tickets for themselves and their families. Originally, my mother was chosen, but I took her spot so she could look after the rest of the family. We have a large family, and we would only have been able to afford one of the last ships out of here, so it was kind of a blessing. What about you?" Nikki replied.

"To be honest, I don't have any family left, and they forced me to do it. Not going to go into all the details, but you taking the place of your mother tells me you must have a big heart. It's both endearing and admirable."

"Don't make me blush. I'm sure you would have done the same if your mother were still around," she said with a smile that made my rat heart melt.

I caught myself thinking about how beautiful her smile was, and I had to shake it off. *You're a rat, remember, and if she knew that, she wouldn't be so kind,* I reminded myself, trying to convince myself that not all humans were like Bob and Jenny. *You will be here far after she goes, and remember what happened to everyone else you were close to. You can't get attached to her—or anyone ever again,* I thought.

"Sorry, didn't mean to," I said, returning her smile with my own. "Do you know how long you have left in here?"

"I think a few more days at most. The first ships are set to leave in a few weeks, and I was a part of the final test group. What about you? Did they give you your ship number yet?" she asked.

"Only a few more days? Well, that's sad. Would have been nice to get to know you with a bit more time," I said, thinking, *How stupid are you? This is perfect. You can't get attached in just a few days.*

She started laughing, and I caught myself gushing over her and her delicate-yet-infectious laugh. I wanted to punch myself to try to knock these feelings out of my brain. *You are a RAT! STOP IT!* I reminded myself over and over again.

"Well, GW, you didn't answer my questions. How long do you have left? And what about your ship number? Maybe we're on the same ship!" she said with a bit of excitement in her voice.

"I don't think that's possible, Nikki. I'm pretty sure I'm on one of the last," I replied, hoping she wouldn't press me on it, as I knew for damn sure I wouldn't be on any ship.

"That sucks! It would have been nice to have someone other than my family to talk to during cryo-breaks. Why don't you clean up after you eat, and we can go for a walk and enjoy the sunset together? I went last night, and it was beautiful," she replied as she got up from the table. As she headed out of the kitchen and up the stairs, she turned to say, "I'm going to get changed while you finish up, and we'll head out."

The food was amazing. I had never experienced spaghetti that had so many different flavors to it. There was a spiciness to it, with hints of garlic mixed in—nothing like the bland red sauce I was used to. It even made me question if I was dreaming, as I didn't remember the food having any flavor the last time I was here.

But it couldn't be, as I never would have imagined a woman like Nikki.

She called down to remind me to do the dishes, and it was exactly what my mom used to say: "Don't you forget those dishes, you hear?"

As I was finishing up the last bowl, Nikki came back into the kitchen with her hair tied up, and her lips had gone as red as the reddest apple. When our eyes met, she twirled around, sending her dress dancing and causing my heart to flutter and my jaw to drop in amazement. The moment she stopped her twirling and smiled at me, I lost my grip on the bowl, causing it to cannonball into the sink, sending water and suds splashing everywhere.

All I could get out was, "Wow."

"Oh, stop it. You're making me blush again," she replied as her cheeks started to go pink. "Let's go for that walk, there's a really nice place to look out from and enjoy the sunset."

Still embarrassed, I fished out the bowl and put it onto the drying rack before grabbing my hat and heading out the door.

Nikki was already a bit down the trail, skipping along with her hands gracefully touching trees as she passed. The trail was familiar, but it didn't hit me until we got to the square clearing as to why, and then I knew where she was leading us.

As I rounded the corner, there it was! The same cliff where Rud and I had last spoken before he and Bissy were taken. It took my emotions for a ride, and before I knew it, sadness was creeping over me.

Nikki turned to me as my eyes started to well up. "I knew it was so beautiful you could cry, but I didn't expect you to. Are you okay, GW?" she said as she sat down on the cliff's edge.

"I'm fine, I'm fine. Just got a bug in my eye is all," I replied quickly, rubbing my eye, knowing all too well I couldn't let her know I had been here before.

Brushing the memories of Rud away, I sat down beside her and changed the topic as quickly as I could, pointing to the mountain across the valley. Luckily, she took the bait and went about showing me the forest and the stream that flowed through it, going on about what a marvelous sight this was to behold.

The real sight to behold was the glimmer in her blue eyes. I had never seen a more beautiful hue of baby blue. It was the distraction I needed to keep my mind from drifting back to my time here with Rud.

We sat there for hours, watching the sun go down and trading stories about our youth. The ones she told of her upbringing in the south were fascinating to me. The food sounded delicious, and her accounts of her partying days were comedic, yet exhilarating. She certainly had an interesting childhood that far outdid my own. Being a human sounded so much more fun than growing up a rat in Tails Falls.

As the evening wore on, I could tell Nikki was getting tired, as her stories kept being interrupted by her yawning, but every time I brought it up, she would brush it off. Clearly, neither of us wanted to leave, especially not me. Her company was a godsend, and I knew that if I were to go to sleep, she would be long-gone by the time I awoke.

Nikki moved closer, pulling my arm around her and resting her head on my shoulder, as the temperature had started to drop. The sun was almost behind the mountain, and as she nestled in further, we both fell silent. I assumed it was because she was watching the last of the sunset but, for me, I was in shock that I was cuddling with a female, let alone with a human one.

Before I knew it, she'd fallen asleep on my shoulder, and I couldn't bring myself to wake her. I slowly slipped out from beside her and picked her up. Carrying her back to the house was easier than I had expected, as she didn't even stir until I had put her into her bed and pulled up the sheets.

"You're a good man, GW; you're a good…" she murmured before trailing off back to sleep.

I caught myself standing there and thinking about how beautiful this woman was inside and out. *Don't do it! Don't get attached!* I reminded myself, but I couldn't help myself, and I leaned down, kissed her on the forehead, and said good night.

On the way back to the house, I decided that I needed to do anything I could to stay awake. I needed more time with her, and if it meant a few sleepless nights, then a few sleepless nights it would be.

Heading back down the stairs, my mind trailed back to her head on my shoulder, and I could feel the smile coming up all the way from my stomach. I'd heard of butterflies in your stomach, but I'd never felt them before.

"Get a hold of yourself! She'll be gone in a few days. You said you wouldn't get attached. Get some coffee, and try not to forget you're a rat," I said to myself in hopes that it would sink in a bit more than saying it in my head.

I was wrong. Sitting at the kitchen table, all I could think about was her eyes, her twang, and the smile she carried throughout all of her stories. I tried as hard as I could not to fall asleep, even slapping myself at one point, but it was to no avail.

My heart sank instantly as soon as I woke up. There was a half-empty cup of coffee still on the table, and somehow, there was a blanket over me, and I certainly didn't remember grabbing either. My heart was racing, and the house was so quiet I could hear my own frantic heartbeat.

Leaping from my chair, I rushed up the stairs and into Nikki's bedroom. *Bed...empty, bathroom...empty.* Her bed was made, and she was nowhere in sight. "No, no, no!" I yelled as I ran back down the stairs, tears welling up in my eyes.

I had slept through her departure. All of that gushing, and I didn't even get to say goodbye.

I sat back down at the table, putting my head in my hands. I felt like a complete idiot for not taking my own advice about not getting attached and for my inability to keep myself awake for even one night.

The self-deprecation was running rampant when all of a sudden, the front door handle jiggled, then turned, and in she walked. I couldn't believe it!

"GW, you look like you've seen a ghost. Did you have a nightmare or something?" Nikki said as she came into the kitchen and put two baskets full of freshly picked berries on the table.

I couldn't even speak. I just got up and hugged her.

"Well, okay then. Clearly, someone had a bad dream," she exclaimed before returning the hug.

After a minute or two, I let go. Regaining my composure, I replied with somewhat of a white lie. "I had one horrible dream, and it ended with you leaving without saying goodbye."

"You sure are an honorable and emotional man, you know that? I don't think I've met a man like you in my life. You carried me home and put me to bed without even stealing a real kiss. Foreheads don't count," she said, giving me a wink that was reminiscent of Rud's.

"I definitely have become an emotional mess over my short time on this planet. I've been through a lot, but the honorable part is probably because I have never kissed a girl before, and I sure wasn't going to have my first be with a sleeping one," I replied, chuckling at how stupid and childish it must have made me sound.

"You haven't even kissed a girl!? Oh, mylanta, GW!" she said with a hint of pink in her cheeks and a look as if she was trying not blush any further.

I was beyond embarrassed; I changed the topic. I asked about the baskets of berries and what she'd been doing out so early.

"Early? It's almost lunchtime, you know? I woke up this morning and noticed that today is actually my last day here. When I came down and saw you sleeping, I grabbed a blanket for you and headed out to get us some berries to enjoy for breakfast. Took me a lot longer than I had hoped to fill up the baskets, though," she explained.

Her last day. I couldn't believe it. *How cruel life is— from the despair of thinking she was gone, to the excitement of her still being here, only to be slapped back to the reality of her leaving again.*

"Guess we'd better make the best of your last day then, huh?" I said, trying to hide my inner turmoil over her departure.

"I'd like that," she said as we both sat down to enjoy a meal featuring the spoils of her morning scavenger hunt.

We didn't talk much as we ate, and only small talk, as the mood had shifted. It wasn't that I was upset with her or her with me, but it seemed there was an unspoken sadness between us.

"Brunch," which Nikki had explained was one of her favorite meals, as it was a combination of breakfast and lunch, was something I had never heard of before, but I too enjoyed it, and vowed to do it more often in the future.

Afterward, we packed up the rest of the food and headed back for the cliff. She wanted to spend as much time as possible enjoying the view before her departure, and said it would be the perfect spot to sit and talk. I agreed without hesitation. There was no place more fitting for last conversations, it seemed. First Rud, now Nikki.

As we started down the trail, we were still sticking to small talk until we got to the clearing. I don't know why or who reached for who, but as we stepped into the clearing, our eyes met the moment our hands closed around each other's. We looked into each other's eyes, but didn't speak a single word. The small talk was replaced by silence as we crossed the grassy opening.

We rounded the corner and stepped out on the cliff together hand in hand. Before I could say a single word, she turned towards me, grabbing my other hand in hers. My eyes met her baby blues just as she leaned in and kissed me. She closed her eyes, leaning in further, pressing her body against mine and bringing my arms around her so I could hold her closer.

I closed my eyes to take in her lips with all of my other senses. They were so soft, and it was way dreamier than I'd ever imagined my first kiss would be.

Until suddenly, as if she had been but a figment of my imagination, she vanished.

Chapter 9

To say that the following few days after Nikki's disappearance were dark would be an understatement. Admitting this is hard, but I tried multiple times to off myself, from attempting to starve myself to jumping headfirst off the cliff.

None of my attempts worked, and I gave up. Instead, I turned to distraction by grabbing the books off the shelf and wasting my time away in bed, only getting up to stretch and periodically go for a run to tire myself out so that I could go back to sleep.

Luckily, all of the books were fascinating, but the *Robotics* trilogy and *Mammalian Anatomy and Physiology* were the ones that made forgetting my misery easier. Humans had done some incredible things by merging what they called machines and mammals, from replacing damaged limbs to enhancing their physical abilities. It was all exceptionally intriguing.

Even though it was incredibly boring, I made sure to spend a good few nights—or should I say years—on the Survival Skills books, as I truly had no idea what I would be faced with when I woke up from this alternate reality.

Will all of the humans be gone? Will the world be the same? Will there be any rats left? I thought. Every time I went for a run, my brain would go all over the place as to what the future would hold after my time here was up. The thought that haunted me, but also gave me hope at the same time, was wondering about whether if Rud and Bissy would still be alive. Vowing to try and find them was the only thing that actually kept me going.

While it wasn't his intention, as I know he only wanted to torture me, I was grateful to Bob for installing the learning software. It made the time fly by and gave me more knowledge and understanding of not only humans, but the world and, most importantly, myself. I was determined to make the best of this knowledge, and when I came back into my room for what would be the last time and saw the clock, its red numbers staring at me and showing *2049*, I prayed I had prepared enough. Who knew what awaited me?

As I laid down in the bed one last time, the fear of the unknown gripped me, almost making me forget to load up the last book on the shelf: *The Aftereffects of Cryo-Sleep and How to Handle Them.*

The day had finally arrived, and I didn't have to wait long before the awakening began. As I sat there staring at my breakfast, my head started to feel fuzzy, my hands flickered, and I could hear a horrendous beeping noise that sounded like it was coming from the back of my skull.

A few short seconds later, the world went black.

The book had said it would be a sweeping feeling of fear, but to me, it felt more like anxiety. It gripped my body, causing my chest to tighten and my heart to race as if it were about to beat out from behind my ribs. The beeping was getting louder, but now, it was outside of my head and coming in through my ears.

This wasn't like the last time I woke up from this; it was slow and agonizing. My body was shivering uncontrollably, and I could feel the sweat dripping down my face from under the goggles as the needles released from my arms.

Something was wrong. The lid didn't pop open like it was supposed to. It made a noise as the suction released, but it only moved about an inch. I could see a sliver of light coming through, but I couldn't push it open. Panic started to set in. "There isn't going to be anyone here to get me out. It's just my damn luck," I said to myself.

As the function in my limbs started to return, I reached up, took the goggles off, ripped the tubes from my mouth, and started pounding on the lid. "Help me! Anyone?"

It was instinct to start yelling, despite knowing there wasn't going to be anyone there. Bob had made that very clear, and Nikki had confirmed it. No humans would even be on earth, let alone at the lab.

After a good twenty minutes or so of hitting the lid, my hands had swollen to more than twice their original size. The shooting pain with every hit was becoming unbearable. It was starting to feel like I was going to break every bone in my hands, but just as I was about to stop, there was a noise from outside.

I questioned if I was hearing things, but it started to get closer. *Is that music? How? It must be! I can hear the rhythmic thump from the bass. Someone is here!*

"HELP ME! Please be real! I'm in here! Please!" I started frantically yelling, as the music seemed to have stopped right beside me, and I could see someone or something blocking the sliver of light between the lid and the rest of the casket.

Relief took over me, and I started to cry when I heard rubble being removed from above me. "I'm not going to die in here. Eat that, Bob!" I yelled as I broke out into fanatical laughter that must have made me sound like a madman to whoever it was who had come to rescue me.

"My name is Niko, dude. I don't know who Bob is, but he ain't here, so he won't be able to eat anything," the voice from outside replied with a chuckle.

They understand me! Dumbfounded, I looked down at my body to make sure I was in fact still a rat. I was, and I still had the same white fur, the same hands, and the same feet, but all of my features seemed larger. *Was I always this size? Have I been in this thing for so long that I can't recognize the size of my own body?*

"Niko!? Name's GW. Looking forward to thanking you when you get me out of here," I replied.

Green fur-covered fingers slid into the crack of the lid, and as it opened, I couldn't believe my eyes . He was a rat with green camouflage fur, like the army fatigues the instructor from the Survival Guidebook had worn. He also had gleaming purple metallic-looking goggles over his eyes and what looked to be black dreadlocks on top of his head. "What's up, my dude? Niko Ratsberg's the name, and musically infused scavenging is my game," the odd-looking rat exclaimed.

I reached out to shake his hand, and before I could say anything ,he slapped it with his palm, then the back of his hand, and then, in one smooth motion, he grabbed it and pulled me in for what was some odd type of handshake-hug. Stunned, I was only able to get out, "Thanks, Niko."

"Don't you mention it there, bud. What the heck were you doing in there, let alone all the way out here?" he inquired.

"Well, it's a long damn story, and I have no idea what you mean by 'all the way out here.'"

"You can fill me in on the way back into the city. It'll be dark in a few hours. I love a good scavenger hunt, but I'm not looking forward to being out here when the sun goes down," Niko replied as he jumped over the casket he'd just freed me from.

Taking a moment to survey the room, I saw that it was nothing like I had remembered it. There were no tables and no rows of caskets, and the white walls were now covered in dirt stains and full of giant holes that the sun was breaking through, sending beams of dust-filled light into its darkened interior. My brain couldn't even imagine what had happened here, but there was no time for that—Niko was climbing out of one of the holes closest to us, and I didn't want to be left behind to ponder any further.

"Wait up, Niko!" I yelled as he popped through the hole and out of view.

As I climbed out of the hole, my eyes burned from the brightness of the sun. It took them a few moments to adapt, but once they did, I found myself looking out over a barren landscape. There were no trees or bushes anywhere in sight, and all I could see was dust blowing across what looked like a desert plain.

Off in the distance, my eyes caught a glimmer of shadowlike structures on the horizon. Niko pointed and said, "That is Gutter City. We've got about two hours to get there. I never hurry for anything, but we're going to have to kick a beat. Wasn't expecting to be digging anyone out of a rubble casket, you know."

Gutter City? Kick a beat? What's up with this guy?

For the first hour and a half, I explained as best I could why he'd found me out there, and I wasn't sure how much Niko was taking in, or if he even believed me. All he would say was "No way," or the odd "Dude." To say he was an odd one would be an understatement. He reminded me of the college stoners from one of Nikki's stories.

The last thirty minutes or so of the journey was filled by me rifling off question after question, but his responses didn't scratch much of the itch for answers. I started with a few easy ones to get him interested, as he'd gone back to head-bobbing to his music. "What year is it? 2050?" I inquired.

"Yeah, dude," he replied, but that didn't give me much to go on, so I had to go with an open-ended question next.

"What is Gutter City?" I asked.

"The city over there," he replied, stone-faced, as if I had simply asked "Where is?" instead of "What is?"

"I got that, thanks. You live there? With who? How many rats?" This time, I added a few sub-questions to try to get a bit more out of him.

"Three thousand rats, three thousand dogs, three thousand pigeons, and three thousand cats."

"Did you just say 'cats?' Like, the animals that eat rats?" I asked, memories of meeting Trix flowing through my brain.

"Dude, they don't *eat* rats. They founded the city. Well, four of them did," he replied as he cocked his head to the side with a look of confusion on his face.

"Well, the cat I met certainly did."

"You're funny, dude. Like two decades ago, when the two-leggers were around, sure."

"That is where I'm from, man. We went over this. You know the part where I said I was in a human lab where they experimented on us?" It was my turn to cock my head at him and receive a look of confusion.

"Yeah, dude. Sorry, man. I spend most of the time vibing in my own head, and kind of zone out a lot."

At least he said it, because I was definitely thinking it. I'd started to wonder if he'd even heard anything I said. He clearly wasn't the rat I needed to be talking to. I was going to need way more information if I was going to survive out here.

"Yeah, I kind of got that. Let's try this one: If you could suggest one person as the smartest person or most history-oriented rat to go to, who would it be?"

"Easy—the teacher down at the Sewer School. Her name is Meg. We can crack on down there tomorrow around lunch. First, though, we got to get through the gates and get some grub. I'm starving."

As we crested the last berm of sand and rubble, the city was finally in full view. There was a concrete wall that stretched for as far as my eyes could see. It was covered in colorful graffiti with some pretty questionable messaging—everything from gang tags to profane messages were strewn all over it. I was in a daze reading what I could make out of it as we approached a metal door with what looked to be a picture of a frog with a big red X over it.

Niko turned to me as he reached for the handle. "Stick with me, and don't look anyone in the eye unless I introduce you. Everyone is cool, but it isn't all cheese and crackers around here. You don't want to disrespect the wrong cat or push a rat the wrong way. I'm not too worried about the other two species, as we aren't on their turf here."

As he opened the door, the hair on the back of my neck stood up and my senses went wild. There were neon lights over almost every door, loud music blared from every direction, and there was a hustle and bustle that I had never experienced before. Then there were the smells—a pungent and somewhat dank aroma, as of a skunk, would waft by every now and again, and yet, when it mixed with the overall smell of the city, it was almost sweet to the nostrils. There were cats talking to rats on porches and dogs playing some sort of dice game with pigeons in an alley; it was too much for my brain to comprehend.

I didn't know what I had been expecting to find when I awoke, but this wasn't it. It was sensory overload. I had never been in a big city before, let alone one like this.

I was doing my best to limit my glancing around so as not to make eye contact with anyone, and I hadn't noticed a rat come around the corner in front of me. We crashed into each other, sending both of us tumbling into the street. *Fuck, I broke one of the cardinal rules*, I thought as my eyes met those of the rat I had unintentionally hit. *Damnit, I broke* all *of the cardinal rules.*

The two teardrops tattooed under his right eye told me right away I was in trouble. He was no small rat, either; his brown fur was popping out from under his gold jacket, which must have gotten dirty from our fall. Turning to me with rage in his eyes, he started to yell at me. "Are you kidding me? My gah-damn gold jacket! You know how much these damn things cost?"

"I…I…didn't see you, man. I'm sorry," I replied, hoping Niko would notice I wasn't behind him and come to my aid. The guy got up and started to walk over to me with clenched fists, his gold chains bouncing and shining in the streetlights as he approached.

Well, you break the rules, you pay the price, I thought as he stepped into the next streetlight. The light caught his hat, and it instantly took my attention away from the impending punch I was surely to be hit with. He had a hat just like my dad's—the one that was taken from me by the humans. I was so distracted that I hadn't even noticed him pull his fist back.

Then, all of sudden, I was brought out of my gaze by Niko yelling behind the man. "Big Lou, don't!" he yelled as the man's fist came rocketing towards me, stopping right before connecting with my chin.

"This asshole with you, Niko!?" the rat called Big Lou replied.

"Yeah. Found this red-eyed weirdo out in the sand dunes on my scavenger hunt today. He says he's from the past; can you believe it? Think the sun has baked his brain even more than mine has been from the jays we've smoked together," Niko replied.

Turning back to look at me, Big Lou's fist unclenched, and his harsh demeanor changed almost instantly. A smile formed on his face as he noticed my dumbfounded stare. "You alright? Are you in shock or something? You didn't even flinch or try and protect yourself," Big Lou said.

The abrupt change in the encounter hadn't even registered yet, as I was still stuck staring at his hat. I didn't come to until he put his hand on my shoulder, which caused me to break from the racing memories and meet his gaze. "Yes, sorry, man. It has been a crazy day in the sun, and, to be honest, I was taken aback by your hat. My father had one just like it, which I lost some time ago. It was everything to me. Where did you get it?" I finally replied.

"This hat? There's a shop on the other side of town called BAF Designs. Mention to 'em that Big Lou sent you, and they will get you sorted. Seriously, though, are you okay? You look like death, and for an all-white rat, that's pretty hard to do, seeing as you already look like a ghost," Big Lou said.

How did we go from him almost destroying my face to him caring about my wellbeing? There was no reason for me to lie, and I knew I would get hyper-focused on things as my brain tried to come back after being in that simulated reality for so long. If Niko thought I was mad, I could only imagine what this guy would think, but I knew that for my own mental state, the truth would be the most liberating.

"I'll be alright, but I have been in a sleep machine for twenty-some odd years, so I'm clearly experiencing what they call hyper-focus. My brain locks onto something it knows, and doesn't notice what's going on around it—or, in the case of me walking into you, it doesn't move fast enough to notice what's right in front of it. Again, my apologies," I replied as I wiped my face and shook my head, trying to shake off the urge to go back to staring at his hat.

"Twenty-some odd years!? Yo, either your brain is fried, or you have some serious stories to tell, and I want to hear them," Big Lou replied before turning back to Niko. "Niko, we need to get this guy back to your place. Get this guy some food and a hot shower. Plus, I have something we can burn down while he does. It's been a minute since we smoked one and caught up, anyways. Can't have this guy walking around dimwitted like this."

Niko smiled and said two words that I would later come to realize had many meanings in Gutter City: "Gang Gang."

It wasn't long after that we reached a small alleyway leading down off the main street. There wasn't much light penetrating its depth, and the music and ruckus from the street started to fade away as we walked slowly down it. I had kept my eyes locked on Big Lou's cap the rest of the walk, so I wasn't even sure how we got there, but luckily, we made it without me causing any more trouble.

His home was at the end of the alley and down a dark flight of stairs that seemed to descend a few stories down below the street. We passed many doors on our way down, but all were boarded up until we finally reached the bottom, where a single door stood with a lone green light bulb above it. It was hard to make out in the green glow, but the sign beside the door read *Deelow and the Scavengers.*

Deelow? Niko didn't tell me he lived here with anyone. To my surprise and elation, I was happy to find that no one else was there when we walked in.

It was a small place, and there were random electronics everywhere, which I could only assume came from Niko's scavenging escapades. There was a small seating area in the front room, a tiny kitchen, and what looked to be three bedrooms with one bathroom just to the left of the eating area. Even with all of the random knickknacks, it was incredibly clean, which I never would have guessed based on Niko's overly relaxed attitude. There was definitely a lot more to this rat than met the eye.

"Shower is in the bathroom, and the towels are behind the door. Don't use up all the hot water, though. My roommate, Deelow, hasn't come home yet. Big Lou and I'll be waiting out here with a surprise for you when you get done," Niko said as he slumped down on the couch, kicking his feet up on the coffee table.

I didn't think twice. Being offered a shower and the opportunity to wash off twenty years' worth of sleepiness and stench was music to my ears.

Standing in the shower with the water pouring over me was exactly what I needed, and taking deep breaths and relaxing my shoulders did wonders for the fogginess in my brain. The day had flown by, and I hadn't really been able to comprehend what was happening. It was almost as if I had been watching someone else live it. I had been warned this would happen, but knowing it and experiencing it were two totally different things. Luckily, the worst of it was supposed to subside within twenty-four hours, and the steaming-hot water was seeming to speed up the process.

The most surprising thing was the lack of thoughts going through my brain. The moment one would start to creep up, it would get washed down the drain by the soothing warmth of the water. Counting my blessings, I finished getting my fur back to its pearly white glory, then stepped out to dry myself off before I used up all the hot water.

The mirror caught my focus as I realized how much larger my features were. Like everyone else here, my body seemed to be a few sizes larger than I remembered. *Is this the DNA-1 serum's doing, or something else? It had to be the serum but that doesn't explain the rest of the inhabitants here. Could they all be descendants of those unfortunate experiments?*

All four of these species had been in there with me. I had seen dogs and cats in the room with Trix and Tex, then the pigeons further down the hall. It had to have some correlation, but if that was, in fact, true, then there were survivors! That meant Rud and Bissy could very well have lived—or maybe even still did—and their offspring could still be here in this very city. But how would I find them?

Realizing I had been staring at the mirror, lost in thoughts of seeing my friends again, I forced myself to finish drying off. A fresh wave of optimism brought a smile back to my face, and I headed out to see what surprise Niko and Big Lou were talking about.

The moment the door opened, I was smacked in the face by a cloud. It was so thick I could barely make out their figures sitting on the couch. As the cloud filled my nose and flooded my lungs, I could smell and taste the same skunkiness from earlier.

Big Lou was laughing hysterically at Niko, who was coughing away. While he seemed like he was grasping for breath, Niko waved me over. "You got to come try this, GW. Big Lou never disappoints. He always brings the best strains," he said between coughs.

"What the hell is it? That's no cigarette," I replied as I slowly felt my way through the cloud towards them.

"You got to be kidding, right? Your eyes are permanently bloodshot, but you've never tried the sweet, sweet sinsemilla?" Big Lou blurted out, only to break out into even harder laughter, which didn't even seem possible.

I don't know why I did it—not wanting to seem even weirder than I already did, I guess—but I lied. "Oh, yeah, of course. We called it skunk back in Tails Falls, but I was too young at the time to try it."

"Well, here you are. Time to pop that cherry," Big Lou exclaimed as he passed me what they referred to as "the joint."

Taking it into my hands, I stared at the wisps of smoke that were curling from the red-hot ember at its end. *Guess there's no turning back now*, I thought as I put it to my lips and pulled. The ember burst with brightness, and I could feel the thick smoke hit the back of my throat, filling my lungs with a heavy, yet tingly sensation. It felt natural, and I relished in it right up until

I exhaled. A scratch formed in my throat, and then I erupted into a coughing fit.

Niko reached over and patted me on the back as tears began to well up in my eyes. He and Big Lou were now laughing like little school children as they both pointed at me. "Atta boy!" Big Lou exclaimed.

Within minutes of hacking up a lung, it hit me—something I had never felt before, and not even remotely similar to how I'd felt when I got drunk for the first time on that dreadful night. It was almost as if my head weighed nothing, and if I wasn't sitting down, my whole body would float to the ceiling. It felt like time had slowed to a halt, but after laughing nonstop for what felt like hours, my eyes started to become heavy. It looked as if Niko, yawning away, was struggling as well.

Big Lou clearly took this as his cue to go. He gave us both a small jab, called us rookies, and said a quick goodbye before heading out the door.

"Alright, man. It's my day off tomorrow, so we'll head over to the school. When Deelow comes in, don't be alarmed—you probably won't even see him, as he's camo-furred just like me. If you do, though, I should warn you: he's a dog, so don't freak out," Niko said as he peeled himself off the sofa, straining as if he weighed a ton.

"Appreciate the fair warning, and thank you again, Niko!" I replied.

"No need to thank me. Get some rest," Niko said, tossing me a blanket before turning off the light and closing his bedroom door.

When he left, it was almost as if all the craziness of the day caught up with me all at once. *What a day*, I thought before falling into a deep, dreamless sleep almost immediately after his door closed.

Chapter 10

"GW, did you see Deelow last night or this morning?" Niko asked as I wiped drool from my lower lip.

"You just woke me up, man. You guys knocked me out with all that smoke last night," I replied.

"Shit. I don't have a good feeling about this. It's not like him not to come home," Niko said with a worried look on his face as he pulled his goggles over his eyes. "Going to have to stop by the yard to see where he went scavenging after we hit the school," he continued.

"Do you want to go there first? We can always go to the school tomorrow," I asked.

"Nah, man. Anyone on his shift wouldn't be back in until later in the day. Let's get going. We'll grab some McGutters breakfast sandos on the way," Niko replied.

The streets were empty, but McGutters was packed. Every booth was full, and you could tell that most of the patrons were worse for wear from the night before. There were even a few dogs passed out at a table, their food sitting there untouched.

Niko ordered us a few breakfast sandos to go, and as we walked out past the dogs, he grabbed a plate of fries right out from under one of their noses. He looked at me and put a finger to his lips, signaling me to shush. I was dumbfounded, but I sure wasn't going to say anything. I was starving.

We walked down 2nd Street, eating in silence. It was still early enough in the day that the streets were pretty much empty of life—no loud music, no yelling, not even the smell of burning weed. It was a blessing to my ears, eyes, and lungs.

We rounded the corner onto Founders' Way and entered a giant courtyard. "Welcome to the city center," Niko said. In the center of the courtyard was a towering fountain with four cats, all perfectly carved out in painstaking detail, as its centerpiece. Walking around it to take it all in, I noticed that there was a plaque at the base of each cat.

"The mysterious four founders of Gutter City," Niko exclaimed before telling me to read the last plaque at my feet.

Whether you're a Cat, Rat, Pigeon, or Dog, gang is gang, it read.

"It was written into Gutter City's constitution as part of the founders' intention, but it hasn't stayed true over the years. Most stick to their own kind, and rats have definitely gotten the short end of the stick since the founders went missing a year or so ago," Niko explained.

"Missing?" I replied curiously.

"Long story, but there are some of us who believe they're still around, watching over us, and if shit hits the fan, they will come back and set things right," he said quietly, waving for me to follow him.

I hadn't believed him when he'd told me that the city was founded by cats, and I certainly wouldn't have believed a rat would speak so highly of them. He seemed to revere them, almost as if they were Godlike. "You know you'll have to tell me this story eventually, right?" I said as I followed him down a small alleyway on the west side of the courtyard.

Similar to the alleyway to get to Niko's house, this one was dark, even in the morning sunlight, and concluded with a stone spiral staircase at the end. Down we went, far below street level. The thrum of the city below echoing up through the center of the stairway with every clockwise lap around told me everything I needed to know about where we were going.

Niko's words played through my mind as we descended. "Most stick to their own kind, and rats have definitely gotten the short end of the stick."

Once we got to the bottom of the stairway and into the street, the scene all but confirmed it. There were rats everywhere, and not a single other species in sight.

What has happened to go from that Cats, Rats, Dogs and Pigeons, gang is gang *sentiment to segregation of species?* I thought.

It was a very short walk to the Sewer School, but that didn't stop me from noticing how many different fur types there were down here. Back in Tails Falls, you had all-white like me, grey like Rud, brown-and-white like Goe, or some mixture of the three colors. Niko's camouflage fur was one thing, but there were so many variants down here that, in the short walk, I had already lost count—there was orange with stripes, blue, purple, pink, camouflage, silver, gold, and even some sort of fish-scale-looking rats. Niko even said there were some neon-green ones, and tattoos had become pretty prominent as well for some of the most gutter of rats. It was fascinating and, for a brief moment, I almost felt a tad bland with my all-white fur.

The Sewer School reminded me a little bit of the school back in Tails Falls, and couldn't have been much larger. The biggest difference was the sports field. Being this far below ground, there was no grass, just a big patch of dirt. It must have been recess, as it was filled with kids kicking soccer balls, throwing footballs back and forth, playing what I initially thought was marbles, but Niko was quick to tell me was actually dice. *Man, what kind of childhood is this, to be that young and already gambling? Do rats really have it this bad that even their kids aren't even able to be kids?*

We entered the school, and my somber demeanor was obviously noticeable, as Niko put his arm around me. "Hey, you ready to find out all the cool shit you missed while you were 'sleeping?'" He made bunny ears with his hands as he said "sleeping," which drew a chuckle out of me.

"You really don't believe me, eh?" I replied.

"Who am I to argue with another man's reality? But seriously, it's a pretty crazy story. I will say I believe that you believe it and to me, that's good enough," Niko said, grinning.

"If you didn't save my life and take me in, I would say you're an 'asshole,'" I said, giving him the bunny ears right back.

"You wouldn't be the first to call me one, or the last, I'm sure," Niko said as we approached a classroom door. "Alright, here we are. We won't have long, as the kids will be back soon."

He didn't even knock, just opened the door and gave the teacher a "Gang, gang," greeting.

"Niko! Long time no see! What brings you down here? Surprised to see you outside of the bar!" the teacher replied as she got up from behind the desk to give him a hug.

"Meg, this is GW. I'll let him fill in the details as to why we're here, but it's great to see you," Niko replied.

The teacher wore a flower in her ear, and her blue agouti fur popped from behind her black-and-gold sweater, but what really took me for a spin was her voice. She sounded exactly like Nikki! She had that same calming southern drawl, tugging at my heart strings and bringing back memories that I had to suppress quickly.

"Pleased to meet you, GW! I know all of the rats here, and yet I have never seen you before," Meg said with a smile.

"The pleasure is all mine. Let's just say I'm new here—to the city and to this time. Niko found me stuck out in the badlands. Been asleep for quite some time,"

I replied ,trying not to give too many details and scare this lady into thinking I was a nut.

"What do you mean, 'asleep?' Don't tell me he found you in the busted-out building? Maybe even in a green box!?" she said with an excitement in her eyes I wasn't expecting.

How would she know that? Have there been others like me? I thought.

Before I could reply, Niko chimed in. "I certainly did. How would you know that?" he replied, puzzled.

Meg walked over to the bookcase behind her desk and started scrolling through the titles, muttering to herself. She stopped on what looked like a very old and distressed paperback. "I have read every piece of literature we have found from the humans who left. You can't be telling me that I'm standing in front of one of the original lab rats!? I have only ever met two before you once ,and I haven't seen them in years. Niko, is this what you found him in?" she replied as she held up a drawing of the sleep pods.

I recognized the handwriting right away. She was holding the Mother of Death's journal! My chin dropped to the floor in disbelief. *How does she have this?* I had so many questions, but I was in too much shock to form even a single word in response.

"Yeah, that's it! Are you telling me he hasn't been spinning tales? He told me he was asleep for twenty-some odd years, and I thought he'd lost a few marbles from being out in the badlands for too long," Niko replied, looking as if he too was going into shock.

Meg was now staring at me so intensely that my shock started to turn into discomfort. Then, suddenly, what she'd said hit me. *She's met two others!?*

"Who were the two others!?" I blurted out, interrupting what she was about to say to Niko.

"I can't remember their names, but their son graduated last year. His name was GJ. Great kid," she replied, still looking at me as if I were some sort of alien.

"Where can I find them? Where can I find their son?" I asked in quick succession.

"To be honest, I'm not sure. They always kept to themselves, but I can ask around. As Niko knows, I have a lot of connections. Come see me at the bar later, and we can discuss," she replied.

"Can you ask around about Deelow while you're at it? He didn't come home yesterday from work," Niko asked.

"Of course. You know where to find me at night. Now, what were you here for again? Got a little side-tracked with this revelation about your friend here! The kids will be back in any moment," she replied.

Putting my hands together in a praying motion, I said, "I was hoping to get some information or books on what had happened, since I missed quite a lot while I was in that green casket. I would love to read that journal as well, if you wouldn't mind."

Meg turned back to the bookshelf, grabbing a thick leatherbound book titled *The Full History of Gutter City*. She handed it to me with the journal on top just as the bell rang to signify the end of recess. "Be careful with the journal. I can't get another copy of it. The other one you can keep, and make sure to come see me at the bar later. We can see what we can find out about Deelow and GJ's parents. Scammy and Lil Hellcat are performing tonight, so I'll make sure to leave two tickets at will call for you!" she exclaimed as the door flipped open behind us and the kids started to file back in. We said our goodbyes and had to swim through a sea of little rats as they funneled back into the room.

Heading back up the spiral staircase out of the gutter of Gutter City, I couldn't stop thinking about what the teacher had said. The two rats she mentioned had to be Rud and Bissy—there were no other females left when I was put under. Rud's last words played through my brain as I thumbed my way through the journal, searching for any notes about them: "I need to be with her and my unborn child."

It has to be them; it just has to be. Please, please be them.

"We're going to go right past the store Big Lou told you about on our way to the yard. Did you want to stop? We still have a bit of time," Niko said, interrupting my frantic skimming.

"Heck yeah, but I don't have any money yet, so we don't have to," I replied, selfishly hoping he would help me out.

"Money—ha! We call them gang tokens. Don't worry about that. I have a few extra you can borrow. You will have to work out a way to pay me back eventually ,though. The only kind of charity I do involves kids, and Meg just confirmed it: you old as dust, bro," Niko said with a chuckle.

"I'm old as dust, but luckily, I don't look or feel it. I'm no charity case, either, and will do whatever I need to do to repay you. I already owe you quite the heavy debt for everything you've done for me," I replied, chuckling right along with him.

Relieved and a tad embarrassed that I had hoped this would be the case, I started to wonder, *How the hell did I luck out to have such a rat find me and take me in? Have the rat gods decided to no longer forsake me or give me a never-ending curse? Can I really be this lucky?*

Just on the corner of Founder's Way and Second Street hung a store sign above a simple red door. It read

BAF Designs. It looked like a simple storefront, but what lay behind the door was far from simple.

As we entered the store, there was the now-familiar aroma of weed in the air. It came from smoke streaming off a blunt in the hand of a huge brown-and-black dog who was sitting on the sofa near the rear of the store. The walls were covered in vintage-looking jackets that you could tell right away were of a quality I hadn't seen in my walks around the city. There were tables covered in pieces of leather, wool, sewing materials, and all sorts of templates. It was evident that this was a true design studio that took pride in its pieces.

"What can I do you for, boys?" the dog asked as he got up from the couch, stretching to his full height and puffing out his chest. He was a monster of an animal. His huge muscles were noticeable even from under his thick black sweater, which had *Gutter* written across it in flames.

"Looking to get a hat made. One of our friends mentioned you would be able to help me out," I replied, trying not to gawk at his sturdy frame.

"Who is your friend? And what kind of hat are we talking here?" the dog asked.

"Big Lou? Wears a gold jacket and a white-and-black baseball cap," I answered.

"Ah, yes, I know him well. Had to fix up his gold jacket the other day. Some asshole ran into him, scuffing up my handywork," he replied, staring at me as if he already knew that the asshole was me.

"I am that asshole," I replied with a nervous laugh.

"I know," he said, still fixating me with a very uneasy glare. "Well, you're lucky he's a better man than me, because if you had run into me, I wouldn't have been as nice." His uneasy glare turned to a smile as he let out a deep chuckle before saying, "Name's Max—Max Gaines. GW the asshole, bring your melon over here and stand on the line in the middle of the room so I can get your measurements."

Startled for a moment as he said my name, I slowly moved onto the line and watched in confusion as Max grabbed a pair of VR goggles off the table in front of the couch. They were very similar to the goggles I had worn in the cryo-sleep machines.

As he slid them on and powered them up, a beam of red light came down from the ceiling and began sweeping back and forth across my head. "What the hell is that?" Niko inquired.

"Scanning his head so I can make a digital trace of his melon. I make all my clothes in VR, so I know the measurements are one-hundred-percent accurate before I print out the stencils," Max replied.

"That is wild, bro. Fucking wild. He already has brain issues. You sure this won't make it worse?" Niko asked with a chuckle.

Once the scan was done and Max was busy crafting the hat inside his goggles, I walked over to one of the many desks. The smell of leather, which overpowered the lingering smoke remnants of Max's blunt, was calling me. I picked up a freshly cut piece and put it to my nose. It was the supplest leather I had ever held or smelled in my life.

As I put it back onto the table, a shiny pair of scissors caught my eye. There was something about them—they looked extremely old, yet brand new.

"Don't touch those," Max's deep voice said, catching me off guard, as I hadn't seen him put his goggles down.

"Sorry, man. They look like quite the tool," I replied, looking up, only to realize he was now right in front of me.

"They can cut a rat clean in half. Want to see?" Max said, the uneasy glare returning to his face.

"No, no, that's quite alright. I didn't mean to touch your stuff; the smell of the leather got me, and there was something about those scissors. I just wanted to hold them," I said, barely able to keep eye contact with him.

"It's quite alright. Those were handed down to me by my mentor, Dante. You see all these jackets? He made these and taught me everything I know," Max said, his uneasy glare turning almost to sadness.

"I was going to say, I noticed those jackets the moment I came in. The quality is something I haven't seen in my walks around the city. He must have been quite the dog," I replied.

"Not a dog—he was a human. He was the greatest designer this world had ever seen, and the greatest human I ever knew," Max replied, a tear starting to form in his eyes.

I was at a loss for words, and all I could get out was, "Wow, Max. I'm sorry."

"Ah, it's okay. The only thing you need to be sorry for is saying you hadn't seen that quality in your walks around town. You almost ruined one of equal quality when you ran into Big Lou the other day!" Max said, a smile returning to his face. "I'll have this hat done by the end of the day. Where do you want it delivered to?"

"Niko, what's your address, man?"

"Any chance you can drop it off to the Notorious Bar and Grill before the shows tonight?" Niko replied.

"Damn straight I can. My man Lil Hellcat is headlining, so you know I'll be there. You buy me a few drinks and fifty, gang, and we'll call it even, yeah? Twenty-five now and the other twenty-five on delivery," Max quickly replied, excitement washing over him after hearing Niko bring up the show.

"I freaking love Lil Hellcat. I guess we shall see you tonight, then. Drinks are on us," Niko replied as he put the twenty-five down on the desk.

We all exchanged a "Gang Gang," and then Niko and I headed back outside. By this point, the streets were flooded with activity, which was a stark contrast to this morning. Street vendors were out hawking all sorts of contraband, and the smells from the food stalls were making my stomach rumble, but we both decided that we would have to hold off from eating until we got to the bar. We needed to get to the junkyard on the other side of town before shift change, so there was no time to stop.

I lost count of all the turns we took and alleys we went down along our way, but after maybe an hour, we ended up coming to the large gates out front of the yard. Niko had explained that we were going to be on the outskirts of Dogtown, but I hadn't put two and two together until this very moment. Looking past the large gate, I could see that almost the entire yard was manned by dogs.

Niko walked up to a small box beside the gate and pressed a button that sent a loud buzzing noise echoing off the buildings around us. "What do you want?" a rough voice asked through a speaker in the box.

"It's Niko! Open up, you old bat," Niko replied, turning to me with a grin on his face.

"I couldn't see your camouflaged ass; I was blinded by the blindingly white rat beside you," the voice shot back.

The loud buzzing returned, and the gate slowly started to open. We walked into the break room, where a half-dozen dogs mixed in with a few rats here and there were getting ready for their shift. All of them greeted Niko with a fist pump and a "Gang Gang."

After making his rounds around the room, Niko leapt up onto the table in the center of the room and yelled, "Any of y'all's sorry asses see Deelow yesterday? Or, better yet, today?"

Everyone looked around at each other, confused, and there were responses ranging from "Nah," to "Fuck no!"

They were all getting into a ruckus, asking all sorts of questions as to why Niko was asking, until the scheduler walked in. Everyone went silent and got back to getting ready for work.

"You guys have two minutes to clock in, or you're all late!" the scheduler said to the group before turning to Niko. "And you—get off the damn fucking table. It's your day off; what are you even doing here?"

This dog was probably even larger than Max, which I didn't even think was possible. There wasn't a sign of a smile anywhere on his face, nor did he look happy to see Niko, regardless of whether he was on a table or not.

Jumping down from the table, Niko replied, "Deelow didn't come home yesterday, and I don't see him here now for his shift. Where was he scavenging yesterday?"

"That's odd. He misses clocking out now and again, but he's never missed a shift in his life. He was supposed to be on the outskirts of Forest Hills between the beach area and Dead Tree Valley," the dog responded with what looked like a glimmer of worry on his face.

Niko didn't even reply or ask any more questions. He just turned and stormed out of the room.

"You tell him he owes me a double shift when you find him!" the dog yelled after him.

I ran after Niko, and luckily, the gate was slow to open, or I may have lost him. There was no way I could have found my way back if I had.

"You alright, Niko? We'll find him, man," I said, hoping to slow him down a bit, as he was walking at almost a running pace at this point.

Niko didn't even turn around or slow down as he responded. "Worst area to send Deelow. We've had a few bad run-ins out that way. That bastard knew that, and he still sent him out there. The Dead Tree Valley is no fucking joke. There are some bad dudes out that way— real fucking bad. If anything has happened to him, I'm taking heads, and the supervisor's will be one of them."

Chapter 11

Niko and I didn't speak a word on the way back from the yard. He was fuming, and he shot down any attempt I made to speak to him.

As we approached the bar, I could feel the nervousness in my chest, as I didn't know what to expect. The lineup outside the Notorious Bar and Grill wrapped all the way around the building by the time we had arrived, and, to my surprise, it was a mixed crowd. Since the bar was in the rat part of town, I had been expecting it to be predominately rats, but there were just as many cats, and even a few dogs mixed in.

We skipped past the line and went straight to a small window beside the entrance. There was a black-furred rat wearing a green beanie behind the glass. He looked to be half-asleep when we approached.

"Notorious said there were two tickets waiting here for me? Should be under Niko," Niko said after startling the poor guy by banging on the glass. He was clearly still fuming from the news about Deelow.

The black rat picked up a clipboard and scanned down what must have been a list of names, stopping halfway down. "Niko Ratsberg, I presume?" the black rat responded, peering over the clipboard to see Niko give a nod. "Two VIP tickets—here you are. Enjoy the show," he said, sliding an envelope through the slot at the bottom of the window.

I could see the anger collectively growing throughout the line as we bypassed it, and I heard quite a few shouts of displeasure as we handed our tickets to the bouncer and walked straight in.

The show wasn't supposed to start for another hour, so there weren't too many people inside yet. The place was huge, with the stage barely taking up a quarter of the open area on the bottom floor. It was bustling with stagehands moving speakers into place and testing the lighting.

While I was busy watching the mic test, someone grabbed the back of my neck. A massive paw wrapped around all the way to my jugular, as if my neck were but a tiny twig. Before I could turn around, a deep voice whispered in my ear as they slowly released their grip. "You better pay attention in here, asshole. You don't want to bump into the wrong person."

I knew the voice, and the "asshole" part gave it away, but I spun around before replying just to make sure.

Sure, enough it was Max, a giant smile on his mutt mouth.

"Not going to lie, your hands are massive, and I almost shit myself, Max," I said, massaging my neck to try to rub off the uneasy feeling of how easy it would be for someone of his size to snap my spine.

"That was kind of the plan," he said as he took his other hand from behind his back to reveal my hat. It was exactly as I remembered it—a perfect replica of my dad's lucky hat. He put it on my head and wrapped his massive arm around me, leading me to the large U-shaped bar wrapping around the back wall of the club, where Big Lou was posted up beside Niko with a drink in hand, laughing his head off, which I figured was either about how scared I looked or how small I was in comparison to Max.

"What are you laughing at, Tiny Lou?" I chirped at him.

"Oh, someone is learning quickly, I see. Backbone starting to form, eh, GW?" Big Lou shot back.

"Don't want to get my neck snapped by a monster like Max here, but I figure I could at least handle you," I said with a playful chuckle.

"I like this guy, Niko. Think we should keep him around," Big Lou replied as he slapped hands with me and brought me in for a hug.

We sat at the bar for a while, shooting the shit and crowd-watching, as the doors had opened and the crowd had started to funnel in. It was getting pretty packed when I noticed a few rats taking bets at the pool table across from us, and I was absorbed into the sly work of one of the scruffy-faced players. He was a blue agouti rat in a pastel color-block hoodie, had won the last few of his games, and seemed to be taking everyone's money, one match at a time. He was clearly pulling a fast one on them all, as he would fall behind early, only to come roaring back to clean off the table. You could tell the crowd was starting to catch on, as a few of the rats were now yelling at what seemed to be the bookie taking all of the bets.

"You watching the dirty pool shark?" Max said as he finished off another drink with a giant swig before continuing. "That's Buffet. Not sure how he keeps this hustle up, but I see him here almost every time I come here, always taking new victims."

"It looks like the gamblers and players are catching on," I replied, not taking my eyes off the raucous crowd that had formed around the bookie.

"Nah, they're just mad at the bookie; this happens every time. Pretty sure they're in cahoots," Max said as he, again, chugged back the remainder of what must have been his fifth drink.

As he turned back to the bar to order another drink, a shoving match broke out between a few of the previous players and the bookie. They were shouting all sorts of threats, but to my surprise, none were aimed at Buffet. He was calmly cleaning the tip of his pool cue without a care in the world while the crowd behind him was calling for the bookies blood.

"Give us our fucking money back! You rigged the odds!" one of the players exclaimed.

"You agreed to the odds. Your time for objection has passed, dear friends," the bookie replied, sending the crowd into a frenzy.

The shoving intensified until a group of rats came crashing into the unexpecting Buffet as he leaned in to inspect his handiwork. It was a terrifying sight, as the impact sent the tip through his right eye. His scream was so bloodcurdling that the entire club went silent. Everyone collectively turned to see the horrific scene as he pulled the cue from his eye socket, taking his entire eyeball with it.

"Holy shit!" Niko yelled as a bouncer came rocketing past us, pushing everyone who stood in his way to the ground.

As the crowd parted with the bouncer's every step, I could see Buffet still staring at his eyeball with his remaining good eye, murmuring to himself. It was hard to watch, but impossible to look away. "My eye! My fucking eye," he kept repeating over and over again as the bookie took advantage of the disgusting distraction and slipped out of the fray as the bouncer arrived.

"Don't think he'll be taking anyone's money at pool anytime soon. Wonder if he'll still be able to play with one eye? Now that's a bet I'd gamble on," Niko said before bursting into laughter.

"Bro, are you serious right now? The guy just lost a fucking eye, for fuck's sake. I hope somebody is smart enough to grab a bag of ice so they can try and save that eye," I shot back.

"Oh, this is the gutter, my friend. I have seen far worse than that, and that was at least an accident," Niko replied, still laughing at his original sick joke.

As I turned back to see if I could catch a glimpse of what was happening, another bouncer stepped into my view, blocking it with his bruising canine frame. "Notorious will see you now. You two come with me," the spotted-fur bouncer said.

"Who the fuck is Notorious? I thought we were here to find Meg?" I asked Niko, but he just turned to the bartender, ordered Big Lou and Max another round, and left to follow the bouncer.

I had to chase after them as they headed towards the stage, stepping over countless rats who were still laying across the floor from being bowled over by the first bouncer. It was like a bomb had gone off, and there were bodies everywhere, luckily all still breathing and none worse for wear except Buffet, who was being carried out on a stretcher. He had a bandage over his eye, and was holding a bag of ice in his lap. My memories of the field med lessons told me his eye was in that bag in hopes of saving it.

The bouncer opened the door beside the stage and waved us through. "Alright, head straight down past the dressing rooms, then take a left at the gold records and let Sleepy know who you are. I've got to get back and help clean up this mess before the damn show starts. Don't you dilly-dally, either—Notorious is expecting you!" the bouncer explained before turning tail and heading back into the crowd.

There was nowhere to stop even if we wanted to. There were stagehands rushing about everywhere, and it was hard enough to stay out of their way as we walked, let alone if we stood still in the narrow corridor. As we rounded the corner to the hallway of gold records, we saw a black and white cat posted up on a chair at the end with a bandit's red bandana around his neck. He looked as if he was sleeping, but as we approached, I could see the green of his eyes shining through his half-open eyelids. *This must be Sleepy,* I thought.

"Niko and GW? Tickets, please," Sleepy said as he slowly stood up.

"Shit. I gave mine to the bouncer at the front door! I didn't know I needed it," Niko exclaimed.

"Those were special tickets with your names on them. I can't let you in without them," Sleepy replied.

"Are you serious right now? What do you want me to do, go back out and ask your coworker for my ticket back?" Niko quipped as he stepped right into the cat's face, the anger from earlier returning to his voice.

"Not co-worker; he's my employee. I run security here, I only report to or work with Notorious," Sleepy replied, not even remotely sounding bothered by Niko's tone or the fact that their faces were inches apart.

"I could care less who you are, bud. Do you know who the fuck—" Niko started, but stopped as the door behind Sleepy opened, revealing the teacher with the flower in her ear.

"Let them in, Sleepy. It's okay. This is a personal meeting, not a formal business one. Tell your guys to come back in when the ambulance leaves and get ready so the show can start," Meg said before turning back to us and giving us a nod to come in.

As we walked past Sleepy, Niko tried to make him flinch by puffing his chest out and lunging at him. Sleepy didn't even react outside of cracking a tiny smile in the most nonchalant way possible. I couldn't believe it. The cat might have looked half-asleep, but he must have nerves of steel and the patience of a saint. I was very happy he did, because I really didn't want to have to fight, let alone with a cat.

The room was dimly lit by candles all over, but it was the wall of TVs displaying various spots of the bar that provided most of the light. Meg made her way over to the desk in front of the televisions and took a seat in a plush leather chair, twirling it a full three-hundred and sixty degrees before pulling herself towards the desk.

It was at that moment that I realized who Notorious was—_Meg_ was Notorious.

I had so many questions, but there was no time for them. We had a purpose for being here, and that was far more important.

"Alright, boys. What information do you want first?" Meg said as she straightened the Notorious nameplate on her desk.

"Deelow, now!" Niko shot out.

"Not even a please!? If I didn't know how important he was to you, I would almost be offended," Meg replied.

Niko hung his head for a few seconds before replying, "Sorry, Notorious. Please."

"As I said, Niko, I know how important he is to you, so no worries. This is personal, so please call me Meg. One of my pigeons says he was spotted being taken in to see King Gutta Gutta. His hands were tied, so you know it wasn't a happy meeting," Meg said. "He never came back out, so it's more than likely that he's being interrogated. I have it on good authority that some strange disappearances have been happening just outside of KGG's territory, so I assume he's taking any unwanted visitors in his hood very seriously."

"Fuck, I had a feeling King Gutta Gutta had something to do with it. Damn yard supervisor had him scavenging out that way, and you know the border lines of these Rat Kings change daily with the ebb and flow of the power struggle. We told them not to send us out that way anymore, but the pickings are too good for them to care," Niko replied, his angry tone turning worried quickly.

"Yeah, but word on the street is Augustus Cheese-ar hasn't been pushing back too much as of late. Seems like both of them are dealing with bigger issues than each other right now. Rumblings from that part of town have been troubling, to say the least. We may be on the cusp of another gang war," Meg said as she turned to look at the screens. "Luckily, it has been quiet around here. Sleepy and his boys do a great job keeping shit in line, and if it does pop off, they're quick to take them outside. Of course, Scammy just hit the stage, so it wouldn't surprise me if another fight breaks out soon."

"I've heard some rumblings, but you know the Gutter—there are very few information sources you can trust. That's why I always come to you. Thank you, Notorious. I mean, Meg," Niko said before standing up and starting to walk towards the door.

"Niko, give me a minute. Do you have something for me as well, Meg?"

"I'll meet you at the bar. I need another drink before we head out. Going to need Big Lou to get us some weed to offer up as a trade for Deelow," Niko replied before heading out of the door, slamming it behind him as he went.

"Don't worry about him. Deelow is like a big brother to him, and he owes him a lot. He brought Niko out of the rat part of town and mentored him into one of the best scavengers around," Meg said before spinning back around to meet my gaze. "So…to be honest, your friends keep a very low profile. I wasn't able to find out anything about them, but I did hear that their son runs with a cat named Jimi Catrix. Both of them have black fur and wear stars-and-stripes bandanas. They should be pretty easy to spot, as you don't typically see cats and rats running together. You should be able to find them on the outskirts of Dogtown, but I suggest you get Deelow before heading out that way."

"Thank you so much, Meg. Seriously, I don't even know how to tell you how grateful I am for this," I said, trying to keep my excitement in check.

"Don't mention it; the pleasure is all mine. When you have some time, we'll need to sit down and discuss what you went through with the humans, though. That will be payment enough for me. The time isn't now, because Niko is going to want to move out of here quickly. Get going, and we'll catch up soon," Meg said as she pointed to a screen showing Niko at the bar, already chugging one back.

Getting through the crowd was a trip in itself. The leopard-furred cat known as Lil Hellcat was coming on the stage, and the crowd was going nuts. Chants of, "Need my scratch, need my scratch, need my scratch," rippled through the crowd. The whole crowd appeared to move as one until the beat started, which sent a surge of energy through it, launching everyone into chaos, pushing each other all over the place and making it almost impossible to get through without doing some pushing of my own. I didn't care who or what I was pushing—cat, rat or dog, if they were in the way or thrown into my path, I was chucking them out of it.

By the time I finally reached the boys at the bar, I was covered in sweat and amped beyond belief.

"What a damn tune, eh? You put in work out there, GW," Max said as I wiped the sweat from my face.

"Not going to lie, that was one hell of a time. I loved every second of it. You're right, too. The song is a banger," I replied before turning to Niko and Big Lou, who were deep in conversation. "We getting out of here, Niko? What's the plan?"

"Just finishing up. We got to roll back by my place to grab a few things, then rendezvous with Big Lou's contact en route. We need to get going before the show ends, or it will take us forever to get out of here," Niko replied.

As we headed towards the door, we could see Sleepy dragging an orange tabby-furred biker rat by the ear. It looked as if the rat's diamond earing was going to rip out under the tension. Noticing us, Sleepy shot us a little smile while pointing at Niko and back to the rat in his paws, as if to say, "This could have been you."

Niko responded in kind with a middle finger and a laugh of his own, which got a nod out of Sleepy. I may have just been making shit up, but it looked like there was a respectfulness to the head nod, which I wasn't really expecting. It was somewhat confirmed, though, as Sleepy reached the door, chucking the rat out into the street and proceeding to hold the door open for us, giving us a little "Good luck," as we passed.

The street outside was busy with groups smoking up and talking shit under the overhang that lined the side of the bar. It had started to rain, so they were all huddled together, while a large puddle had formed at the edge of the sidewalk, and it was half-filled by the soaking rat that Sleepy had just thrown out. Even though he was half-submerged, his eyes were glowing a crazy blue that I had never seen before, and he had one devilish grin on his face as he reached into his biker vest and pulled out a gold dog-bone chain.

How ballsy must this rat be not only to start a fight with a dog, but steal his damn chain?! I thought right as the door burst back open.

"Grab that fucking rat! I'm going to kill him," the dog standing in the open door yelled. I could almost see the smoke coming out of his ears, he was so hot with anger.

The rat was halfway down the block by the time I turned back, and there was now a group of dogs chasing him.

"Pretty sure his name is Bo, but I could be wrong. What I do know, though, is that if they catch him, he's as good as dead. But, knowing those biker rats, he'll slip away clean and make a few bucks hawking that chain at a pawn shop," Niko said, starting off in the opposite direction from the chase.

As the rain continued to pelt down around us, the noise off the roofs hanging out over the sidewalk was somewhat soothing. Coming up to Second Street, we ducked under another overhang, and I noticed a flyer that seemed to be pasted all over the light posts and shop windows. It read *Frog Fighting Championship— this weekend*, and there were two pictures of some angry-looking frogs and their corresponding fight records below them. It made me wonder how this was possible, as I remembered seeing anti-frog spray paint on the city walls when I first arrived. My curiosity was definitely peaking, and something inside me made me feel uneasy about it.

"Niko, what's the deal with these frog fights?" I said as we ran for the next overhang.

"What do you mean? They're frogs, and they fight!" he said without hesitation.

"I get that, but I noticed some anti-frog graffiti around town, and didn't think much of it until I saw these flyers."

"Oh, yeah. You will read about it in the book Meg gave you, I'm sure of it. But the frogs from outside of the city are banned. Only the fighters are allowed in, and that's just because most people around here are degenerate gamblers," he replied as he grabbed a paper off a table out front of the store overhang we were under. Putting it over his head, he darted out into the street and headed for an alleyway.

I was dying to know more. My gut was screaming at me that this was something important, but we were moving faster now, and it wouldn't take us long to get back to Niko's place at this pace.

Hopefully, I'll be able to catch up on some reading after we find Deelow, I thought as we slipped into another alley.

The rain picked up the moment we entered, making Niko's makeshift umbrella completely useless. "Bloody hell," he said angrily as he threw it to the ground in disgust. It was then that we both gave in and accepted that were going to get soaked, no matter what we did to try to avoid it. Our shoulders slumped at the same time as we walked on, surrendering to the pounding rain.

We arrived back to Niko's place absolutely soaked through to the bone. The franticness of the night was washed away by the puddles we had become. We grabbed some towels and collapsed on to the couch.

A few moments later, the phone rang, and Niko sluggishly picked it up. It was Big Lou. His contact had called off the drop-off, and we would have to wait until tomorrow to try to get Deelow.

"Get some rest, GW. We can't go until tomorrow now. The storm is getting worse, and the contact won't go out in this weather," Niko explained as he got up from the couch and started heading for his room before turning around to say goodnight.

I would have been lying if I said I wasn't relieved. That walk in the rain had taken everything out of me, and this was going to give me a chance to get some reading in as well. After a quick shower to warm up my bones, I kicked my feet up and cracked open then Gutter history book.

It didn't take long to find what my gut was telling me to look for.

Chapter Two: The Frog King Betrayal

In the first three years of Gutter City, frogs were not only a part of society, but they were revered for their prowess in the boxing arena. It didn't take long for the Frog Fighting Championship to become a staple in gutter culture and to cement its place as one of the longest standing pastimes for all species. It was put on weekly by the frog king named BaCroak, and the rats were in charge of taking care of the bets.

With every week, the wealth and power of BaCroak grew, and his influence in the political structure of the Gutter started to rival some of the founders. It ended up going to his head and brought on an attempt to over-

throw the political governance of the city by attempting to assassinate one of the founders. The plan was to have a servant rat take out a council member so BaCroak could take his seat. In turn, he would make sure the Rat Kings would rise up out of the sewer and climb the totem pole of influence.

On the day before the plan was to take place, a courier pigeon for one of the Rat Kings overheard a few frogs discussing the plan and discovered BaCroak's true intentions. Not only was he planning to betray his alliance with the founders, but he also planned to double-cross the rats by pinning the nefarious events solely on the Rat Kings.

Upon hearing this news, the Rat Kings went straight to the founder's council. At first, they were met with skepticism, but it's believed that they were advised to prove it by carrying out BaCroak's plan. The counter plan went off without a hitch and it's believed that they faked the murder and, when King BaCroak came to the council, he was apprehended and held for trial.

The founder's council hasn't been seen in public since the execution of King BaCroak and the banishment of the frog king's son and loyal subjects. It's believed that the frog community has taken refuge beyond the Dead Tree Forest. Outside of the fighters, no regular frog has ever stepped a webbed foot back into the city.

The Rat Kings were paid for their loyalty by being put in charge of the Frog Fighting Championships and awarded the right to bring fighters into the city for the events. It's currently not known how this recruitment process works or what arrangements have been made between the Rat Kings and the fighters that allows these events to continue, but they've run uninterrupted for years.

As I closed the book and my eyes for the night, I thought, *This explains the anti-frog graffiti, but it doesn't explain why my gut is screaming at me that this is so important.*

Chapter 12

We stood on a corner just outside of the city center, awaiting the arrival of Big Lou's contact. It was a blazingly hot day without a cloud in the sky. Any signs of yesterday's storm were rapidly evaporating, causing the humidity to rise so high that I felt as if I was soaked just as much as I had been from the rainstorm the night prior.

Thankfully, we didn't have to wait too long. A silvery rat in a neck brace came out from the alley across the street and waved us over. "Oh, fuck me. This asshole sent Tiny!?" Niko said as he stepped out onto the street.

"What? You really don't like many people, huh?" I remarked.

Niko stopped me in the middle of the street and said, "No, no, I like this guy. He's good shit. Only problem is, he never stops laughing and please, *please* don't ask about his neck brace. Poor guy woke up in that state one day and has no idea how he got it."

"Like amnesia?"

"Worse—barely remembers anything, especially that night, and every time I see him, he has a new story as to what actually happened. It's kind of comical, but we really don't have time today," Niko explained with a chuckle before continuing into the alley.

"Niko! What's good, bruv? Been a minute. Sorry I couldn't meet you last night. You know I can't get this cast wet," Tiny said, followed by a laugh that was so infectious that I couldn't help but laugh myself. "Who the fuck is this guy? You think I'm funny, bruv? What, you never seen a rat in a neck cast or some shit?" he barked as he stared me down with a straight face, which completely threw me for a loop, since he had just been laughing like a hyena.

"No, no, man—no disrespect. You got a great laugh, and I couldn't help but join ya," I responded, and was relieved to see his expression instantly change back to a smile.

"Well, let me tell you, this cast ain't no fucking joke, you hear me? I got it fighting a few dogs down in Dogtown a few weeks back. You should see them—fucked them up right good," Tiny exclaimed before turning to Niko.

I was completely confused at this point. Niko had just told me he didn't know what happened.

"You got my money, homie?" Tiny said as he looked around the alley to make sure no one was around to listen or see what was going down.

"Of course, man. Do you need me to count it?" Niko replied, pulling a bag of gang tokens from his backpack.

"Nah, bruv. I know where you live. I'll pull up to your back window when you're smoking if it's short. You know I'm not coming to your front door—you know I don't do stairs since those damn fucking birds pushed me down a flight, putting me in this damn cast!" Tiny replied as he took the bag and handed over another bag, which was so stinky my nose was taken over the second he pulled it out.

My confusion was turning to complete bewilderment now. *Did this guy just tell us two different stories about how he got this neck cast in a matter of seconds?*

"Yeah, I remember. Did you ever find them yet to repay the favor?" Niko replied.

"Nah, not yet, but when I do, you know they'll be in full-body casts, if not in caskets," Tiny exclaimed before losing it in laughter again.

"Hey, you know if you do, you can count on us for some backup," Niko said, then hit me in the chest as if to tell me to agree. He didn't have to, though; I had just met this guy, but I could already tell he would be one hell of a good time to be around.

"You know it, Tiny; we may be somewhat strangers, but any friend of Niko and Big Lou is a friend of mine," I chimed in.

"I'm going to hold you two to that. God knows I can't take on those damn cats alone. I know the color of the car they hit me with, and I'll find it!" Tiny said. He gave us a "Gang Gang," and turned back down the alley from which he had come.

Wow, three different stories in one conversation? I can only imagine what smoking with this legend would be like. I know our paths will cross again, and I can't wait until that day comes, I thought as Niko and I just looked at each other and laughed before heading back out into the street.

It was hotter than all hell, and we adopted a very similar strategy to the rainstorm the night prior, only walking on the shady side of the street and ducking under any store overhangs when we couldn't. As we approached the edge of town, we stopped under a large oak tree to discuss our plan of approach.

Niko wanted me to keep quiet and let him do the talking, only answering if I was asked a direct question, and not to give any information as to where I had come from. The plan was for us to walk up to the guards and demand a meeting. If we snuck around and were caught, it would only end up with us in the same situation as Deelow. If they didn't allow the meeting, then we'd have to resort to Plan B: return to this tree and wait for nightfall to try to infiltrate and extract Deelow.

"You don't want to make them think you have anything to do with these disappearances or to raise any unneeded questions that may derail our goal of getting Deelow out," Niko reiterated.

"My mouth is zipped shut, so no need to worry about me. Let's go get your brother back!" I said, physically making the motion of zipping my mouth shut to reaffirm my understanding.

As we rounded the last corner onto Gutta Avenue, the state of the street showed that we were indeed on the outskirts of town. There were overgrown bushes and trees lining the road, as well as all sorts of trash, including tireless cars, many of which had been burnt out or stripped all the way down to their shells. At the end of the street stood a large warehouse that looked just as unkept as the street itself. There were *No Trespassing* and *Private Property* signs everywhere, and if I didn't know better, I would have sworn it was abandoned.

As we rounded the corner of the building, we were startled by a voice coming from behind us. "You boys lost or just stupid? We don't take to kindly to visitors around here," the voice said.

Turning around, we were met by a group of rats holding all sorts of blunt objects for weapons. If we had not been expecting it, I probably would have run, but Niko had made it clear that this was going to happen, and this was our chance to demand the meeting.

"Neither lost nor stupid. We're here to demand a meeting with King Gutta Gutta. We have business to discuss, and we won't discuss it with lowly gang members like yourselves," Niko replied, causing me to cock my head in shock at his boldness. We certainly hadn't discussed insulting the security pack.

His statement was met with a few head tilts before an eruption of laughter, as they surely didn't expect to be met with a stone-faced insult either, let alone a demand.

"Well, we were going to give you the chance to leave, but if you want to sign your own death certificates, who are we to stop you. Follow me. You can wait in the lobby while I bring your disrespectful demands to the King, and he can decide your fate," one of the bigger black-furred rats said, stepping from the middle of the group and walking past us.

Surrounded by the group of menacing henchmen, we were led inside. The moment we stepped through the doors, it was as if we were stepping into a luxury mansion, not an abandoned warehouse. The floors were polished, without a speck of dust to be found. Cushy, ornate sofas and furniture were set up in such a fashion that the large open space felt like an intimate social club.

It was the last thing I would have expected, but it did make some sense, since this was the home of not only a King, but one of the people who would have benefited from the wealth that the former King BaCroak once enjoyed. The posters of past fighting champions said it all.

It didn't take long before we were led out of the main hall and into what looked to be like a training room, but my attention went straight to the boxing ring in the center of the room, where two giant frogs were going at it. They were so large that I almost thought they were toads at first.

If this was some sort of practice match, it sure didn't seem like it. Their punches were so heavy that I could feel the *thud* from every landed blow. It was quite the spectacle, and it was easy to see why this pastime was so revered by the habitants of Gutter City. The larger of the two was sweating profusely, which was what I'd attributed to the smell of dirty pond water wafting through the room, while the smaller opponent didn't even have a bead of sweat on him.

As we circled around the ring, the bell rang out, and a strong voice yelled out to stop the match. "Take a break, boys. We'll pick this back up after I'm done with these two stupid rats," the voice said. I couldn't see them yet, but it had to be the King.

"Are you kidding me? I was just about to knock this oversized fly-eater down. Look at him—he's tired as all hell. I told you, size doesn't matter to me; I need some damn competition," the smaller frog responded, while turning to give us our first look at the crown-wearing black-furred rat named King Gutta Gutta.

As my eyes started to move away from the smaller frog, I noticed his massive back tattoo. It was a combination of all sorts of odd tribal symbols that circled around the letters KBC with a crown at their center. *It has to be a reference to King BaCroak, but if it is, how is this frog even allowed inside the walls of the city? Something doesn't feel right,* I thought, but the King was now walking towards us, and I just had to log it away.

"Listen, when I say it's over, it's over. I've got business to attend to; you can knock him out and have your next victim shortly, but until then, go rest," the king said before finally turning his attention to us.

The frog slammed his fists together in disapproval of the order, but got out of the ring and started to walk out of the room, making sure to punch every heavy bag on his way out before ripping his gloves off and chucking them down in anger.

"He is a feisty one, I'll tell you that much, and if you don't have a good reason for wasting my time, I'm going to make the both of you be his next victims," the King said as he eyed us both up and down with his one good eye. I hadn't noticed that he had a patch over his eye, nor that he was wearing a black turtleneck, as they both blended right into his black fur. "Don't you both speak at once now; I don't have all damn day."

"I hear you're holding one of my friends hostage, and I've come here to make a deal for his release," Niko said, sticking to his plan of keeping small talk to a minimum.

"Direct and to the point, I can respect that. First, tell me: who gave you this information?" the King responded, not taking his eye off Niko.

"Irrelevant. The only thing that matters is that I have brought an offering for his release and a guarantee that we'll never scavenge anywhere near your territory ever again," Niko snapped back.

"Ah. See, you only get to become a king and stay one by knowing that nothing about information gathering is irrelevant. Who was it? Augustus Cheese-ar's spies? Or maybe that nosey bar witch?" he asked, his eye still trained on Niko as if he could read his thoughts and body language.

"Neither. A bird said he saw him when he was doing his rounds of checking on the scavengers for the scheduler. I overheard them discussing it at the yard. Needless to say, the scheduler wasn't going to try to save him, and so it falls to me as his brother," Niko said, stone-faced. Even though I knew it was a lie, he said it so quickly and with such a conviction that there was no way the King would know any different.

"Interesting. What are you offering, and why should I not just take it and let the frog take his anger out on you and your brother?" the king replied.

"I know you respect a rat's word and candor, so that's the only reason I can give you for why. For the what, I have a pound of your competition's best weed, along with the seeds for the exact strain, so you can plant and distribute your own," Niko responded, taking the bag out and waving it around so the smell would take over the room.

"I must say, I do like your style, but I'm going to need more than that. I do have an idea, though; I'll need you to take something for me to Augustus Cheese-ar. He won't trust one of my own, so maybe he'll accept it from a third party like yourselves. If you succeed and return with his response, I'll free your brother and let the three of you walk out of here," the King countered.

"I won't say no to that. Just tell me what and where it needs to go, and I'll get it to him. You have my word," Niko replied without hesitation.

"Give me a moment, and I'll get you everything you need. Do not break the seal of the letter I give you, or not only will I kill your brother, but I'm sure Augustus will kill the two of you for reading his mail," the King said before walking out of the room, leaving us alone.

I waited a few moments to make sure the coast was clear before speaking, just in case anyone was still in ear shot. "Did you see the tattoo on that frog's back?" I inquired. Niko just turned and stared at me. "You didn't see the KBC with a crown over it mixed into the tribal designs?" I pressed again.

Niko just raised a finger to his lips to tell me to be quiet. I looked around, confused, as I couldn't see a single soul in the room. After I'd returned my eyes back to Niko, he pointed upwards. Following his finger to the ceiling, I noticed a silhouetted figure move out of view from the skylight in the roof. Someone had been watching us, and it clearly wasn't one of the King's men.

As I looked back at Niko, the door opened, and the one-eyed king returned with a sealed envelope and the guard who had brought us in originally. They looked as if they were brothers, but you could tell that even if they were, the King didn't treat him as such.

"Take these two back out to the street, and bring me back some McGutters while you're at it," the King said to his black-furred minion. "I expect you two to be back here no later than tomorrow at this time with his response. If not, the deal is off, and I'll make sure your brother is never seen again. You hear me? Now get going. Tick-tock," he said to us as he handed Niko the letter.

We both nodded and headed back out into the blazing hot sun. Our escort left us at the end of the road without a word, and we went on our way.

We stopped back at the Oak tree to get some shade and discuss our next steps. "Who do you think was up there? It couldn't have been one of their own, or they wouldn't have ducked away when we noticed them," I asked.

"I have no idea, but they were clearly eavesdropping. Maybe it was, as the King said, one of Augustus's spies?" Niko said before moving on to, as he put it, more pressing matters. "We've got to move fast; I know we have until tomorrow, but I want to get this done today. I don't want Deelow to spend another night in there. Plus, if I'm not back to work by tomorrow night, I can pretty much count my ass as unemployed. Same plan as here, except this time, we can't make demands, and I'll have to watch my mouth. Augustus is a tad bit more civilized—or, should I say, *refined*."

Niko was soon moving fast, but, thankfully, the sun had gone behind the buildings at this point, and there was a nice cross-breeze, making the trek a lot easier. If he'd kept this pace earlier, I think I would have died from heat exhaustion.

As we approached what Niko called the territory line, I saw a distinct difference in the cleanliness and upkeep of the surrounding buildings. It was progressively getting cleaner, and shortly after crossing over an old set of railway tracks, it was as if we were in a whole different city. There was no graffiti on the walls, no garbage in the streets, and it was incredibly quiet. No loud music or shouting could be heard anywhere.

After spending my first few days surrounded by the hustle and bustle of the inner city and the sewer, it was almost surreal to be back in a place that somewhat reminded me of Tails Falls. True, the buildings were huge and made of concrete and brick, but the feel was much of the same.

As we cut through a small park, it felt as if someone was watching us. It was as if a shadow was bouncing between the trees on the outskirts of the park, but I could never catch a glimpse of what it was.

We reached the street, and our shadow seemed to disappear as a dark black car pulled up and stopped directly in front of us. I couldn't see who was inside, as the windows were tinted as black as a starless night. I tried to get a look inside as the passenger-side window came down a crack, but Niko stepped in front of me and approached the car.

"State your name and your business here," I could hear a deep voice say.

"Name is Niko Ratsberg, and this is my friend, GW. We have a message we need to deliver to Augustus. Might you please point us in the right direction?" Niko replied.

The window rolled back up and the back door opened, causing Niko and I to give each other a puzzled look.

"I guess we're supposed to get in?" I said, to which Niko just shrugged and ducked into the back seat of the car.

As we got in, the door closed behind us, and we didn't even have time to sit down before the car started moving again. We both fell into the seats, still puzzled as to what was happening. Niko tried to talk to the figures in the front seat, but there was another piece of tinted glass in between us, so they either couldn't hear us or had no interest in talking.

It was pitch-dark inside, and even the bright sun couldn't penetrate through the glass, to the point that I couldn't even see out to the street. At first, I started counting the turns in hopes of being able to recount the trip in case we needed to run, but it wasn't long before I realized that was going to be impossible. It was as if they were taking us in circles, doubling back every few turns and even pulling U-turns at times to throw us off. They definitely didn't want us to know where we were going or how we got there.

It took us a good forty-five minutes before we finally slowed down to a crawl and then a full stop. I could hear what sounded like a large metal door close behind us, and once it hit the ground and locked, our door was finally opened.

As I stepped out into a bright garage, it took my eyes more than a few seconds to adjust. It was as bright as the white walls of the lab room I had been imprisoned in for so long, and it made the hair on the back of my neck stand up. In front of us stood a trio of suit-wearing rats with blank expressions on their faces, and neither Niko nor I knew what to make of it. Even he was speechless.

Luckily, someone must have called into suited rats' earpieces, as they put their hands to their ears and put an end to the awkward starring contest. "Right this way, gentlemen. It looks as though the King will fit you in before his next meeting," one of the rats said, stepping aside and gesturing to a door behind him.

We were led down a long hallway until we reached a large, wooden door that opened up into a tropical greenhouse. The smell was incredible, with many wild-flowers and lush green plants that I had never seen before. There was even a small stream running through it, filled with tiny goldfish that sparkled under the babbling water and added to the calming nature of the space. We were then led through a bamboo-lined walkway that brough us out into a circular cobblestone courtyard with small stone benches around its exterior. The far side featured a large waterfall that must have fed the streams we had passed.

Sitting in front of it all was the King himself. Augustus Cheese-ar, with his gold fur, gold teeth, and matching gold crown, sat peering over his sunglasses at us as we approached.

Before we took our seats across from him, Niko looked at me and then back to the king before bowing his head slightly. I mimicked his bow and took my seat beside him. I figured this was his attempt at being more civilized, but it was met with laughter from the King, so it clearly didn't work.

"Bowing? Are you here to pledge allegiance to me or give me a message? Don't mock me with your fake formalities," the King said, disdain emanating from his voice.

"My apologies, sir. We were sent to deliver a message from King Gutta Gutta," Niko replied, causing the guards to reach inside their coats for what I could only assume were concealed weapons.

The King raised his hand, and they returned to their positions with their hands behind their backs. "And what would this message be? I know you're not a part of his crew—or are you so newly initiated that I'm unaware?" Augustus inquired.

"We're not a part of his crew, nor will we ever be. He has one of our friends, and we were asked to bring this message to you and return with a response in exchange for his release. We don't know what's in this letter, so please don't hold us responsible for its contents," Niko replied, almost stuttering with nervousness.

"Ah, the scavenger dog. That makes a bit more sense now. I was wondering what a scavenging camo rat was doing out in my part of town and not on the other side of the wall, digging through relics. Hand over the letter. No harm will come to you, no matter the contents," Augustus said with such a calm demeanor it was impossible not to believe him.

He seemed so calm, cool and collected for someone of his stature in society. It wasn't what I would expect of a king, and was a stark contrast to the power and authority King Gutta Gutta had exuded. I'm sure the settings in which the meetings were held contributed to these feelings, but both men were clearly kings for their own reasons. Both were at the top of the rat food chain and held the largest swaths of territory, which butted up against each other, causing the ongoing power struggle between them.

It all made me wonder what this letter contained and what it might mean for the rats stuck in between these two warring Kings, let alone for the city itself.

Niko handed the letter to Augustus. He promptly examined the red wax seal for any signs of it being tampered with. It bore the markings of a crown with two boxing gloves hanging below it and GG flanking the leathery mitts.

Augustus was still peering over his glasses, moving his eyes quickly between the two of us, as he put his thumb under the seal and began to open it. It was only milliseconds before his calmness seemed to waver and his cool and collected facial expression changed. He seemed to reread the letter three or four times before taking his glasses off and wiping his forehead. Reaching into the neon-green belt bag that he wore across his chest, he pulled out a gold Zippo and proceeded to light the letter on fire, dropping it on the ground in front of us as the flames took over the last of the parchment.

"King Gutta Gutta didn't tell you what was in this letter? And you didn't read it, correct?" Augustus asked, clearly still flustered by its contents.

"Correct, sir. Our instructions were not to read it, only to give it to you, and to return with your sealed response. He made it clear that there would be dire consequences if we breached this agreement," Niko responded.

As one of the suited guards leaned in and whispered something into Augustus's ear, I noticed movement overhead. Peering up, I could see that same silhouetted figure looking down at us through the glass ceiling. When Augustus returned his glasses to his face and stood, the shadowy figure vanished. "The two of you will have to wait here. I have another meeting to attend to, and after that, I'll return with my response," the King said before turning to walk away.

"Sir, we don't have much time. We need to return in haste. Is there any way we can take care of this before your next meeting?" Niko said with a desperate tone in his voice that made the king turn back around.

"This isn't something I can take lightly, and as much as I understand your predicament, I wear the crown here, not you. You have my word that I'll be back within the hour. If there's anything you need in the meantime, my men here will be happy to provide it," Augustus said, calm returning to his voice as he pushed his glasses up and walked away.

Niko was obviously not very happy that we had to wait, but I tried to assure him an hour wasn't bad at all, and we would indeed get Deelow out today. There was no getting through to him, though; he just sulked away through the bamboo, and I knew better than to follow him. Outside of the silent treatment he'd given me and the small angry outbursts, he'd been pretty unflappable throughout this whole ordeal. I knew I'd said it before, but I was incredibly lucky to have found such a friend— or, should I say, lucky that he had found me.

I thought for sure Augustus's suited henchmen would keep an eye on us, but shortly after the King and Niko had walked off, they beelined for the door outside. I could see them through the glass lighting their cigarettes and talking amongst themselves. They couldn't have cared less what we were up to, so I figured I would explore and take in the different tones of green foliage and multi-colored flowers.

The greenhouse itself was way larger than I had originally thought, and the path seemed to wind off in every direction. I stuck to following the pebbled path that meandered beside the babbling stream until my nose caught a whiff of a plant that I knew was a staple in any Gutter garden. It was impossible not to follow the smell, and as I came up to a plastic curtain covering a doorway, I stopped.

There was a shadowy outline of someone moving behind the curtain, but I couldn't quite make out who or what species it may be. They seemed to have heard me coming, and were moving quickly away from the opening.

As I peeled back the curtain, all I could see was a sea of green swaying left and right with the wind from the fans above. It was so thick that I couldn't see past the first row of plants, and there was no one in sight. "Where did you go? You still in here?" I called as I started to push a few plants aside in hopes of seeing further into the room.

As soon as the plants parted, there was a quick burst of wind that startled the heck out of me and sent me tumbling over. A brown pigeon bolted out from the field in front of me and through an open skylight in the ceiling.

"What the hell was that? Was that the shadowy figure that was looking down on us at the warehouse? The same one that followed us all the way through the park?" I sat questioning myself until Niko interrupted me.

"Get up. You shouldn't be in here. If they catch us in here, who knows what they're going to think?" Niko said as he put his helped me off the ground.

"Did you see that? Did you see the pigeon?" I asked, brushing myself off.

"Yes, I did. I think your assumptions may be right, but why would it be following us?" he exclaimed.

We walked back through the curtain and straight into two henchmen's chests. They were both staring at us, clearly not impressed.

"We didn't touch or take anything, unless you count the amazing smells we enjoyed," Niko said, adding a little chuckle in an attempt to lighten the mood. The henchmen didn't laugh in return, and proceeded to pat us down to make sure we weren't hiding any stolen buds.

After realizing that we were empty-handed, the one with the earpiece said, "The King is almost ready. You should return to the seating area before he returns, and I would advise you don't mention that you stepped foot in his private stash room."

That was easy advice to take. We didn't want to prolong this any longer than we had to, and we certainly didn't want to anger a King.

We didn't have to wait long; as soon as we sat back down on the bench, the King came out from behind the waterfall and took his seat across from us. I could see a letter sticking out from his chest bag, and I couldn't help but notice the seal. It was simple compared to King Gutta Gutta's, although I could tell what his stood for. This one was simply a bunch of grapes on a vine, and it had me wondering what the symbolism could mean.

I didn't think about it too long, though, as the shadow flew over us, causing everyone to glance up, including the King, but by the time we looked up, there was nothing there.

"Alright, gentlemen. I know you're in a rush, so I'm going to have my boys drive you back and drop you off at the end of Gutta Avenue. I don't need to remind you that the contents of this letter are only for King Gutta Gutta's eyes, and I trust you will give me the same courtesy you gave him by keeping this sealed," King Augustus said before handing the letter over to Niko.

"Oh, and for your troubles, here's something for you to celebrate with your dog friend on his release. I know KGG, and your friend will definitely need this after being in his merciless hands." Niko and I were stunned, but we nodded as he handed us each a tightly rolled joint before cracking a smile and giving us a few last words before walking away. "I trust these will make you forget this exchange ever happened."

My mind was abuzz as we got into the car with thoughts of what could be in these letters and endless theories as to why that pigeon was tailing us. It made the drive back very interesting, but luckily, it was a lot quicker this time, as the henchmen took a direct route. I wasn't sure if it was because they were no longer worried about us or they had just gotten sloppy. Either way,

King Gutta Gutta's comment about intelligence gathering never being irrelevant made me log the turns in the back of my brain just in case we ever needed them again.

As promised, the henchmen dropped us at the end of the road, and the moment we stepped out onto the street, they peeled a quick U-turn and sped off back in the direction of their own turf.

The sun was getting low in the sky at this point, but there was no denying that we had plenty of time to get Deelow out, and the look on Niko's face said it all. He was grinning ear-to-ear, and the pep in his step was infectious. "Time to get Deelow out and celebrate! Let's do this!" I said, looking over at Niko with a grin of my own.

"Damn straight. Same plan as before—no talking!" he reminded me as we rounded the front of the warehouse and made our way towards the doors.

Before we reached the stairs at the foot of the doorway, the doors burst open, and to our surprise, it was the King himself, with no guards flanking him or anywhere to be seen. "Well, I'll be damned. You two are quick. I trust you have something for me?" the King yelled down to us.

"Yes, we do. We met with Augustus and gave him your letter. If he didn't make us wait for his response, we would have been back a while ago. Where is Deelow?" Niko responded, his joyful tone gone, replaced by the cut-and-dry attitude he'd put on earlier.

"Straight to the point. I sent the boys down to go get him when I saw you get out of one of Augustus's cars on the security cameras. He'll be out here any minute. Now, the letter—give it to me!" the King quipped back.

"No disrespect, but you can have it when my brother is beside me. I have learned one too many lessons from being too trusting, even when it comes to my own kind," Niko replied, causing me to cringe, as even after all we had been through to get this far, it could all go wrong at any moment.

"You're one ballsy son of a bitch, and I respect that. If I didn't already have enough mouths to feed around here, I would offer you a job. So be it," the King said before pulling out a walkie-talkie. "Bring him out."

Within a few seconds, the doors opened again, this time a crew of rats filed out with what had to be Deelow. He was shorter than most of the dogs that I had seen so far, and you could tell he was worse for wear. His right eye was so bruised that it was almost completely swollen shut, while the monocle he wore over of his left eye was cracked right through the middle. They definitely had given him quite the beating while he was in there. He had camouflage fur that was very similar to Niko's, and it initially hid some of his mass but as he started past the crew of rats it became more evident that what he lacked in height was made up for in muscle mass. It made me wonder how these rats were able to capture him let alone be able to hold him, it had to be a sheer numbers game that did him in.

Niko tried to run past the King to Deelow, but the crew of rats were quick cut off his path and push him back down a few steps.

"Let him go! We did what you asked, now, let him the fuck go!" Niko screamed.

"Ah, ah, ah—not so fast. You're still holding your end of the bargain in your hand. Give it to me and the three of you can go on your merry way," King Gutta Gutta replied.

"Here, take it," Niko said, shoving the letter into the King's hands.

The King turned to his crew snapping his fingers, causing one of the rats to cut the rope around Deelow's paws loose. Before the rope could even hit the floor, Deelow and Niko had made it to each other and joined in an embrace that would even make a cold cat's heart melt. It wouldn't surprise me if Niko's goggles were filling with tears at this point.

"Alright, gentlemen. Keep your lovefest for once you get the hell off my turf. I respect the bravery and appreciate the discretion, but it's time for you to move on out of here. Oh, and remember: never fucking come back around here again," King Gutta Gutta exclaimed before turning to signal his crew to follow him back inside.

To say I was relieved this ordeal was over would be a complete understatement, and I could only imagine how Niko and Deelow felt. It felt as if the gods were smiling down on us, as the sunset was streaming oranges and yellows across the sky as we walked side by side down the street, joints in hand.

We had finally done it. Deelow was free.

Chapter 13

The next few days were a welcome reprieve. I tended to Deelow's wounds while Niko was at work, and we sat around chatting in the clouds at night. It amazed me how quickly I had become indoctrinated into the smoking culture here; it seemed as if everyone and their grandmothers did it. I wasn't complaining, either, as I had never laughed as hard in my life as I had the past few nights. Deelow was downright hilarious, and we had become fast friends. It was incredibly easy to see why Niko admired him so much. Not only had he pulled him out of the sewer, he had done it without any ulterior motive.

Similarly, throughout all of our conversations, he was genuinely interested in my life story, my upbringing, and my long and twisted journey to today. It wasn't just surface-level small talk, either; he wanted to know all of the details and how I felt I had grown from the experiences I had encountered and endured. He was infatuated with my stories of what happened with Bissy and Rud, and vowed one night to do everything he could to help me find them.

"So, you're telling me that Notorious told you she thinks they're still alive, and instead of going to find them, you stuck with Niko's crazy ass to come find me?" Deelow inquired as he passed me our third joint of the night.

"To be honest, I thought about leaving to go find them, but I just couldn't do it. Niko had taken me in and treated me like I was his kin, very similar to what you did for him. It just felt like the right thing to do. You know what I mean?" I replied.

"I certainly do. Shows you're a man of good character, my friend. So, now that I can see out of both eyes again, are we going to go out tomorrow and try to find these two legends, or what?" he said enthusiastically before turning to Niko, who was busy rolling up another one. "You got day shift again tomorrow, bro, or you going to join us?"

"The scheduler has me on a double tomorrow to cover for your bitch ass, so I won't be able to come, unfortunately. Found a stash of old robotics that's going to take me a few days to haul out. You sure you two don't want to give me a hand?" Niko asked.

I thought about it for a millisecond, as I hadn't had any chance to utilize my robotics knowledge since waking up, but it was only a brief lapse, as Deelow set me straight with his reply. "No way, homie. We're going to Dogtown tomorrow to see if we can find any info about GW's lost homies. Plus, I haven't seen my brother in over a year."

"Doubt he's going to want to help you, man. That dog despises you, and you showing up with another rat is going to set him right off. Actually, I wish I could be there to see his reaction," Niko said before breaking into another round of laughter.

"You aren't lying, but it still doesn't change the fact that he's my brother. You just worry about carrying all that metal, and I'll worry about Zane," Deelow quipped back.

I came to realize that this was how most conversations went here—jabs and barbs with no malice intended, but if one showed any weakness, they would grow in intensity. I quite enjoyed it, as it bred confidence in one's ability to take and give back the subtle aggression. At first, I had been put off by it, and thought everyone here was angry or super insecure, but I now saw it as a part of an aggressive culture that was founded in the hardships each species had endured since the departure of humans. Gutter City wasn't for the faint of heart or the weak-minded, but I loved it.

Niko had left before we woke up the next day, but had left a few coupons for McGutters breakfast sandwiches on the table for us, along with a note that read, *Be safe out there, boys. Oh, and give Zane a hearty "Fuck You," from me, will ya?*

"Does Niko really hate this guy's biological brother?" I asked. Deelow just laughed it off, but I was itching to hear the backstory.

It was a lot cooler of a morning, and the stench of the city was slightly subdued because of it. It was even cold enough that there was steam coming out of the sewer vents, making the morning sunrays dance off the street clouds.

After we had grabbed our chicken sandos from Mc-Gutters, I brought the subject up, and it was anything but a short story. "Eh, yo, whatever happened between Niko and your brother to cause such disdain for each other?" I asked.

"Oh, man, don't bring it up to Zane, even though I'm sure he will, but it's more about Zane and me than Niko and Zane. My little brother and I had a difficult upbringing, as our parents passed shortly after arriving to Gutter City. It left us scrounging on the streets at a young age, and even after our situations slightly changed, he never really wanted to grow out of that life. He's always felt slighted by this world, and as I got older, it started to hold me back. Shortly after I started working at the yard, I moved myself out of Dogtown to try and better my situation, and even then, I offered for Zane to come with me. He chastised me for it and said I was turning my back on my roots, as if I was too good for Dogtown or some shit. He didn't understand that I wanted more, and I didn't want to be considered just a Dog; I wanted to be a part of the community as a whole. He hated that, and even more so when I hooked up with Niko. When I first met Niko, he reminded me of myself—a positive light in a negative situation. He wanted more from life, to do better for himself and others at all costs, but he didn't have a gang to his name. We hung out for a few days, and I offered him the same offer I gave to Zane, but instead of chastising me, he jumped at it gratefully. I found him a job at the yard, and he's worked his ass off every day since, not just to repay me, but to be a better rat. You know what I mean?" Deelow explained.

It was a lot to digest, and I didn't know what to say right off the cuff, which was enough of a pause for him to continue.

"Seeing him bring you into the fold without questions isn't even surprising to me. Niko would give the shirt off his back to help people, and it makes him the complete opposite of Zane. They've only met each other a handful of times. Zane has never shown him an ounce of respect, and has looked down on him for not only being a rat, but for his positive outlook on life. Zane just hates seeing people be successful and happy. Deep down, though, I think he really just hates himself and misses our parents. You feel me?"

"I get it completely. I lost my dad at an early age, and my mother, which I still can't really talk about. You think he'll ever come around?" I said, still trying to digest it all, and hoping that he didn't bring up my own issues over my mother.

"I hope so, but I wouldn't put money on it at this point. Wait until you meet him. You'll understand," Deelow replied, thankfully not bringing the questions back to me. We were approaching the gates to Dogtown, and he was busy outlining what to do. It wasn't anything new, though, as it was the same shit Niko kept telling me: shut up, don't speak unless spoken to, and stick close to him.

There was a large decrepit wooden sign that went across the street, signifying that we were entering Dogtown. Shortly after crossing the border, the brick road quickly turned into gravel, the dust puffing up from around our feet with every step. The buildings got increasingly smaller and transitioned rapidly from brick to wood construction as we walked further in.

It had the same feeling of neglect and lack of wealth the sewer inhabited by the rats had. To me, both places were physical representations of how the Gang is Gang sentiment from the history book had slowly died and how the discontent of the lower species had grown from its decomposing culture and perceived inequality. The further I went outside of the city center ruled by the cats, the more this became evident to me, and the more it seemed more likely that it would culminate into another gang war between species.

"Deelow, I've been reading up on the history of the city, and wanted to get your take on what happened to the Gang is Gang culture. It doesn't go into the details of the gang wars or even how they ended," I said, curiosity getting the better of me.

"That is because they never fully ended. There was a time, albeit a brief time, where the money distribution was more equal, and the opportunities for anyone, no matter their species, were abundant. In my eyes, it went south when the frogs were banished. Some dogs felt as if they should have been put in charge of the fights. I also think that because the founders have been reclusive since then, it has bred rumors around who is running the city, and each species feels slighted by the change in the flow of money. It used to spread throughout the city, but you may have noticed that outside of the rat Kings, the sewer is in shambles, and outside of the yard owners, Dogtown has fallen into disarray," Deelow replied.

"I can understand that, and can definitely see the similarities between the sewer and Dogtown. What about the pigeons? There isn't much about them, nor have I seen where they live yet."

"Oh, yeah? I'm surprised that there isn't more in there about them. They live on the rooftops in and around the city core. I tend to think of them as rats with wings, but a heck of a lot less trustworthy than the rats I've met. They spin information to their advantage, and have made quite a good life for themselves trading information to the highest bidders. You never know who they're working for these days or what their motives are, so I tend to steer clear of them altogether," Deelow replied.

"Interesting. There seemed to have been a pigeon tailing Niko and I when we were going around trying to get you out. The first time I saw him was when we first got to the warehouse, and he followed us to Augustus's mansion, but I haven't seen it since. Any ideas as to why they would have been following us?" I asked.

"What color was it?"

"A brownish-beige color. I didn't get a good look at it," I answered.

"Well, it for sure wasn't Notorious's bird or we would have heard about it, then. Maybe one of the rat Kings'?" Deelow replied.

"Hmm, don't think it could have been one of the rat Kings," I said, and was about to continue when the door to the gym we were passing flew open, almost hitting me in the snout.

A familiar face came out laughing their ass off. "You got reflexes, GW! Thought for sure I was going to catch you with that one!" Max Gaines said, wiping his sweaty face with a towel in the process.

"Bro, you almost killed me, and I wouldn't have expected that from someone who cares so much about their work, that shit would have ruined my damn hat!

What the hell is going on man?" I replied before stopping him from hugging me after our handshake. "You're sweaty as fuck; don't you even dare."

"Ah, you wear your hat backwards, anyways. Your schnoz would have taken all of the beating, saving my handiwork. What the heck are you doing out in Dogtown, man? You're really getting around, eh?" Max replied, still laughing.

"Max, you know Deelow?" I said, gesturing to him beside me.

"Damn straight, I do. What's good, big dog? I thought that was you, but was too focused on this bleach-white little man. You look like they did a number on you. You here to rally the troops for retribution?" Max said to Deelow as they clasped their monstrous hands together. The two of them were clearly two of the most muscular dogs around, as even the dogs in the gym were staring at the two bulging figures blocking the doorway with envy in their eyes.

"I'm doing good, man; I'm sure no one here even lifted an ear after hearing I was locked up by a bunch of rats. No need to rally any troops, and especially not for any type of retribution. I got business to attend to. You see my bitch-ass brother around lately?" Deelow said with a hint of anger in his voice.

I hadn't thought about how he must have felt knowing that two rats were the only ones to come looking for him. None of his childhood friends or family had—just his adopted rat brother and a rat he hadn't even met yet. That had to sting, so I could understand where the anger came from. And Max definitely didn't help the situation.

"Yeah, I ain't going to lie to you—your brother and his boys cracked quite a few rat jokes about you. I ended up punching one of his boys at the bar when they took it too far. You know how they are, though; they didn't even try to fight me for doing it, the pussies. That was the last time I saw your brother, and you know he's probably at the trailer. That bum doesn't do shit except smoke, drink, and sit on his damn porch, telling anyone who will listen how the cats are holding us down or that they're the ones causing dogs to go missing lately," Max replied.

"You're good shit, Max—a true brother. You see a black cat and a white-and-black rat, both with stars-and-stripes bandanas, around here lately?" Deelow inquired.

"Not in a while. I used to grab protein shakes with a little extra in them from the cat. Believe his name was Jimi, but haven't seen them in a minute. Shit's been really weird around here the past week or so," Max said.

"Wait, did you say dogs have been going missing? Is that what you meant by it being really weird around here?" I interrupted.

"Yeah, man. I think five or six dogs have gone missing in the past week, all at night. Most people won't even go outside when the sun goes down because of it," Max replied.

Could it be the humans have returned? Are they taking victims for new experiments? It sounds exactly like how it all started back in Tails Falls. First some of the two rat kings' men, now dogs from Dogtown. Something terrible is coming, I can feel it... My mind trailed off.

"So, rats are going missing, and now dogs!?" I blurted out. I wanted to bring up the humans, but didn't want to sound like a lunatic.

"Didn't know about the rats. That's fucked up. Zane thinks it's the cats. Watch what he says when you tell him rats have been going missing, too. Hit me up when you two get back into town. I got to head back to the shop for the next week, so I'll be around. Stop in so we can catch up, Deelow. It's been too long," Max said as he wiped the remaining sweat from his brow and walked back into the gym.

"How the hell are people going missing everywhere? It seems as if it's happening on the outer edges of the city, and hasn't made its way into the core, but why?" My mind was a mess, and my stomach was so uneasy, it felt like there was a rock in my gut.

Deelow and I walked the rest of the way to his brother's trailer in silence, and I was so lost in my own mind that I didn't even realize we were walking through an entire park full of trailers. It was as if I was in a haze of depressive memories, replaying the fateful nights that destroyed Tails Falls, stole my youth, and killed my family and friends.

I snapped to only after Deelow started yelling his brother's name as we approached a derelict-looking trailer. It was tucked away from all the other trailers, and looked as if it had been abandoned some time ago. Beer cans and cigarette butts everywhere were the only signs that life still took place here.

It didn't seem like anyone was home until we stepped around to the front of the shack on wheels. Slumped over in a lawn chair was a brown-and-black-furred beast of a dog who had the same stars-and-stripes bandana around his head that Deelow wore.

As we approached, Deelow gave me a shushing gesture before taking a few steps closer and screaming like a banshee into Zane's ear. The unexpecting dog fell ass over tea kettle off the chair while sending the half-drunken beer that was in his hand straight into the sky, causing a beer shower on the two of them as Zane tried to put his soul back into his body and figure out what was happening. I could see the color come back to his face the moment he realized it was his brother laughing hysterically in front of him.

In the blink of an eye, though, Zane tackled Deelow to the ground, clouds of dust puffing up around them as they rolled back and forth, each trying to gain the upper hand. Deelow was laughing the entire time, even as Zane took shots at his rib cage every time he saw an opening.

It looked harmless until it wasn't. Zane rolled away, picked up an empty wine bottle off the ground and broke it over a burnt-out barrel. Holding up the jagged end in his left hand, he lunged and pointed it at his older brother.

"You really want to do this? Do you not remember the last time you pulled a bottle on someone? I would have thought you would have known better by now, after that cat almost took your damn eye out, leaving you with that ridiculous scar over your eye. You do also remember that I'm your fucking brother, right? I know you're trashed, but come on," Deelow asked.

I hadn't noticed, but Zane's right eye had three deep scars going from just above his brow all the way to his cheek. It was clearly a cat's claws that had done the damage, which was probably one of the main reasons he blamed cats for so much of his pain.

I could see the moment his inebriated brain computed what Deelow had said. His eyes went from an angry haze to confused in two seconds flat. He looked at the bottle in his hand, back to Deelow, and then back to the bottle before releasing his grip and dropping the makeshift weapon to the ground. "Deelow!? What the actual fuck, man?" Zane said, shaking his head and wiping his eyes in an attempt to rid himself of the remaining drink-induced fog.

"What the actual fuck, indeed. You really got to cut back on the drinking, man. I know I scared you, but does that really justify a stabbing?" Deelow replied, still laughing.

"Reflexes. Not all of us live in a peachy inner-city neighborhood, brother. Why are you even out here? You finally got released by those rats? You love them, and they lock you up. What a joke," Zane said, the anger returning to his eyes.

"You want to know what a joke is? Not one of you dogs even lifted a paw to help me. Niko and a rat who had never met me before risked their necks to get me out. I gave you an opportunity to get out of this neighborhood, and you didn't take it, so don't even start with me on that, either," Deelow snapped back.

"Fuck Niko!" Zane exclaimed.

Deelow replied, "Yeah, he told me to say fuck you, too!"

They went back and forth for almost an hour before we all finally sat down to get to business. I sure as hell wasn't going to get in-between the two of them to try to speed things up.

After we took our seats around a makeshift firepit, the conversation finally turned towards what we had actually come here for.

"Do you know anything about a cat named Jimi who hangs around with that black-and-white rat? They wear the same bandanas as us, so I figured you would know them. I've been told they spend a lot of time around Dogtown," Deelow asked.

"Yeah, I know them. Why are you looking for them?" Zane replied.

"Does it matter? Where can we find them?" Deelow replied, causing Zane to squint angrily at the two of us.

I didn't want the conversation to derail back into trading barbs, so I chimed in. "The rat is the son of my two best friends, who I haven't seen in years—"

I had started to speak before Zane got up and started to walk into the trailer. "Deelow, want a beer? My head is pounding," he asked, not even acknowledging that I had been speaking, or that I was even there, for that matter.

I just stared at Deelow, my white fur practically turning red from anger. I was furious that Zane would disrespectfully ignore the fact that I was speaking, let alone not offer me a beer. It bubbled over quickly, and I lost it. "Are you brain-dead, or just a full-blown disrespectful and ungrateful piece of trash? Get us both a damn beer while you're in there, and hurry up. We don't have all day to waste here," I snapped at him.

Zane looked at me like I had just punched him in the face, while Deelow just gave me a smirk and a nod. I hadn't meant to snap, but I also wasn't going to let some drunk disrespect me like that, even if he was Deelow's brother.

He came back outside with three beers, though, so it was worth it. He made sure to toss me mine with some extra force, but I was ready for it. "Appreciate the cold one, Zane. Where was I? Ah, yes. I'm looking for the rat's parents. They're old friends of mine," I replied after cracking my beer and taking a nice chug.

It took him a while to reply. He looked as if he was still in shock from my outburst, as he just sat there looking at his unopened beer for longer than he should have. "They used to help me run some of my bootleg moonshine, but they stopped showing up a few months back when they got on their own shit, making and selling some pump mix to the jocks down at the Gutter Gainz gym. Your best bet is to go up Kibble Hill Road and check the basketball courts. They always used to be up there," he finally said.

Deelow had told me about Kibble Hill Park one night while I was dressing his wounds. He used to play ball up there until late into the night, as it was the only park that had lights. All the dogs and their families would be up there barbequing and shooting the shit in the summer months. It reminded me of my youth, as all of the big town events during the summer were held at the school's football field in the middle of town.

"You want to roll up there with us, Zane? We can challenge someone to a game of pickup for old times' sake?" Deelow asked.

"Nah, man. I've spent enough time with you today. Take your rat friend and get the fuck out of here," Zane barked back.

Deelow broke into laughter. "You know, GW here's got you pegged—you really are a disrespectful and ungrateful drunk. I'll swing back through after we find his friends so me and you can have a little chat, brother to brother. Try not to destroy your liver or piss off the wrong cat again, you hear me?"

"Don't bother, brother," Zane barked before tossing away his empty can and giving us the finger as he walked back inside.

Deelow just looked over at me, shrugged, and said, "Come on, then. At least we got what we came for and my conscience is clean."

It had been such an unreal encounter that I was left kind of bewildered, even with all the warnings from Niko and Deelow. Growing up as a single child, it had always been my dream to have a brother, but this made me question that.

My heart was racing with anticipation as we walked up what seemed to be the never-ending hill that was Kibble Hill Road. My legs were gassed, but the thought of being so close to seeing Rud and Bissy again made it easy to tolerate the discomfort. The music and shouting from the top got louder and louder with every step, and as I crested the top of the hill, the bass nearly knocked me off my noodles for legs.

The park was jammed, mostly with dogs, but there were random cats, rats, and even pigeons mixed into the crowd. There were raucous games of basketball on every court and crowds of people sitting around shooting the shit, barbequing meat, and, by the sight of all the smoke, enjoying their fair share of joints. I even saw one group passing around what looked to be a joint that was the size of my arm.

If people were worried about the missing dogs, you wouldn't have known it with all the laughter and carefree activities going on.

"Ah, good old Kibble Hills. Hasn't changed one bit," Deelow said. After sticking his noise to the sky and taking in a deep breath, he patted me on the back and led me into the chaos.

Deelow was a popular dog in these parts. He was frequently approached and pulled in all different directions as we walked through the crowd. We decided to split up so I could survey the crowd while he tried to gather information from the people who were trying to get his attention. He was here to help me, but seeing how excited he was to see so many of his old friends, it felt wrong to ask him to put that aside to help me have the same feeling.

I ducked and weaved through the crowds, my eyeballs working on overdrive, making sure I didn't miss looking at a single face. After passing through the field of tents and barbeques, I moved towards the courts, where the games were in full swing. As I walked through the crowd on the hill overlooking the courts, I noticed a brown pigeon that looked exactly like the one that had tailed us. The moment our eyes met, I knew it was him.

He recognized me immediately, and before I could take another step, he bolted, running straight through an ongoing game, colliding with a dog who was about to shoot, causing everyone on the court to stop and stare at him. He said something to them, which I assume was an apology, before taking off into the sky.

It didn't seem as if he was here for me, so why the hell did he run? But before my brain could even compute what happened, my eyes set a light bulb off in my brain.

Standing right beside where my eyes locked onto the bird was a black cat with round green sunglasses shining in the sunlight. He was wearing a stars-and-stripes bandana. It had to be the cat I was looking for, but was he talking with the bird, or was it just coincidence?

I glanced around quickly to see if I could flag down Deelow, but when I found him, he had his back to me, and was busy talking to a group of dogs. There was no time to wait for him. If this was truly Jimi, I needed to go before he had time to leave.

"Your name Jimi?" I asked the cat as I calmly walked towards him.

He pulled his circle glasses down to look me in the eyes and said, "Who's asking?"

"Name's GW. I've been looking for you and your friend. Where is GJ?" I said, instantly kicking myself internally, as telling someone you've been looking for them and inquiring about where their partner in crime is may sound kind of suspicious.

"Who the fuck are you? You working with the air patrol or some shit? I thought they only employed narc-ass birds?" Jimi snapped back, fists clenching at his sides.

I put my hands up to try and calm the situation and said, as fast as my lips would move, "No, no, no. I'm an old friend of Rud and Bissy's. I'm just trying to find them, and I was told that if I found you and GJ, then I would be able to find them."

He flicked his glasses back over his eyes and grabbed me by the arm, dragging me away from the crowd, which had turned and begun staring at us after he said the words "air patrol."

"If you knew Rud and Bissy, you would know better than to speak their names in public like that. Who the fuck are you? You have ten seconds to explain yourself, or I swear, I'll drag you down to the forest and kill you myself," Jimi said as his claws slowly began exposing themselves from under his paw's fur.

At this point, the tough façade I had learned to brandish in situations like this crumbled. My focus was so fixed on his shimmering claws that it wouldn't surprise me if I was visibly shaking.

"Hear me out, okay? This is going to sound crazy, but I knew Bissy and Rud from our childhood in Tails

Falls, over twenty-odd years ago. We were all captured by humans and put through unspeakable experiments before we got separated. I woke up from one of those experiments in this place, confused, and I thought for sure that everyone I knew was long dead. It was only after meeting a teacher in Ratsville and hearing about GJ and his parents that I had any hope of seeing them again. I have been looking for you guys and praying to the rat gods ever since." I was surprised I was able to get that much out, even though I was stuttering throughout most of it.

Jimi looked shocked. His mouth had dropped about halfway through my explanation, and still hadn't closed. "There's no way! White rat, red bloodshot eyes, grey-and-black backwards hat and white tank top, with GW as his name. How is this even possible?" he said, looking even more rattled than I had been when his claws came out. "How are you alive? I've heard stories about you my entire life. Even my own father told me about the day he met you and almost ate the three of you."

Did he just say his dad almost ate me? There's no way. Could this really be Trix's son? "Your father's name is Trix?" I asked.

"I can't believe this. Yes, my father's name was Trix. Him and my godfather Tex passed a few years after we arrived in Gutter City, so Bissy and Rud took me in and raised me as one of their own. The hairs on the back of my neck are standing up. This is so creepy," Jimi explained.

"My hair is also standing up. I can't believe Tex, Bissy, Rud and even your father made it out of that lab alive! I have so many questions," I replied, absolutely gushing with emotions.

"Well, there's no time for them right now. I need— oh, sorry—*we* need to get back to the bunker ASAP. I'm only here to get some barbeque to bring back to GJ and Bissy," Jimi said, suddenly sounding overwhelmed and rushed.

"What about Rud? Is everything okay?" I asked, sensing something had shifted, and it wasn't just his hurried demeanor.

"I don't know how to say this, or if I should even be the one to tell you, but Rud passed a few weeks back, and Bissy is very ill. I'm only here to get food to bring back. We need to get going *now*," Jimi said as he ran off back to the group of dogs he had been standing with. I hadn't noticed, but he had been in line at a barbeque stand, and was obviously waiting for the food he'd been sent to acquire.

He grabbed a bag off the table and told me to follow him. I tried to get him to wait for me to get Deelow, but he was now sprinting ahead. "There's no time! I'm already late," he yelled back to me.

I ran after him, leaving Deelow without a word.

Chapter 14

Rud is dead. I don't even know how to feel right now.

A few weeks ago, I'd thought everyone was dead. Then, there was hope they were alive, and now, I'd come to find out that he was gone. There were no words that could explain how mixed-up my emotions and thoughts were.

Jimi was too far ahead for me to talk it out with him, to put the pieces together before seeing Bissy again. *Pull yourself together. If she's unwell and just lost Rud, she needs you to have it together,* I thought over and over as I struggled to keep up.

We were running in the opposite direction from the inner city to the west end of Dogtown. I had no idea where we were or where we were going at this point, but I couldn't have cared less. I finally caught up to Jimi at the end of Kibble Hill Road, only to find that we were at a dead end blocked off by a massive barb wire fence. There were signs all over it—*Do Not Enter*, *No Trespassing*, *No Dumping*, and an ominous *We Are Watching*—but oddly, there were no buildings or houses in sight.

Jimi looked around as if checking to see if the coast was clear before he dipped behind a thick cedar hedge that stood to the right of the fence. There was a small trail that led along the fence line and opened up to a ridgeline overlooking the city. It seemed as if we were at the highest point in Gutter City, aside from a few of the taller buildings in the city center. I could see everything from up here, from Dogtown to the Rat Kings' territories, and almost the entire perimeter of the city walls, from the Dead Tree Forest to the desert wasteland where Niko saved me.

After the trail turned left into the forest, Jimi stopped again to look around. *Who the hell is he looking out for? No one followed us, and we're in the middle of nowhere at this point,* I thought as I watched him duck behind a very large oak tree that was just on this side of the fence line.

"Jimi, what are you doing?" I asked after a few moments of odd silence. I walked closer to see if I could hear if he was taking a piss break or something, but it was dead quiet.

"Jimi?" I said again before peering around the tree to find nothing. He'd straight-up vanished.

I was about to yell for him when something in my peripheral vision dropped down out of the tree, landing directly behind me. Before I could turn around, a wing wrapped around my chest, stopping me from being able to run, while another slid over my mouth, stifling my ability to yell for help.

"Shhh. Do not yell; do not scream. I'll take my wing away if you promise not to yell," the mystery bird whispered. I nodded in agreement, and the bird loosened his grip and released the wing from my mouth.

I slowly turned around and came face-to-face with the brown pigeon. My mouth dropped open, and I was about to spew out a hundred questions when his wing slid over my mouth again to stop me. "I said, 'Shhh!'

Look at the backside of the tree. Do you see that knot in the center?" the bird whispered.

I nodded again.

"Press it and push in," he said again in a hushed tone.

As soon as I pressed the knot, I could feel a latch behind the bark release. *A secret door?* Pushing it inwards revealed a spiral staircase within the trunk of the tree, and I stepped in with the pigeon following behind me. As the door closed behind us, lights appeared on every other step.

I could hear Jimi talking to someone below as we started our way down. They were yelling at each other. "I told you to hurry the hell up, Jimi! You know she's unwell and needs to take her meds with food. You can't fuck around and mess up her schedule!" the voice speaking to Jimi said.

"You don't understand, GJ. You aren't going to believe who's coming down the stairs behind me. This will brighten Mother's mood, I guarantee it!" Jimi responded.

He is talking to Rud and Bissy's son! My emotions hit me like a ton of bricks, and I almost burst into tears. *I'm actually going to see Bissy again, right now.*

"What the hell, Jimi? You know she doesn't want visitors, and of all places, you brought them here!? Late with her food, *and* you've gone against Mother's wishes? What's going on with you?" GJ screamed back at him as we rounded the last few stairs and into their view. They were standing in a small room with giant metal doors on each of the three outer walls.

GJ glared at me with confusion as Jimi spun the wheel on the door behind him. I could hear gears spinning within it before four metal rods retracted from each corner, releasing the door from its shackles with a clank. Still grasping the wheel, Jimi leaned into it and slowly started rolling the massive door inwards.

With every inch, my heart raced faster and faster. Sweat starting to clam up my hands in anticipation. It had been over twenty years; would she recognize me? Would she be happy to see me? I was about to find out, and my heart felt as if it would explode if the door moved any slower.

GJ was still staring at me as Jimi waved me in. I was so nervous that I was rubbing my palms together so hard the skin was almost peeling off. My heartbeat had leveled out, but was still at a borderline anxiety-inducing pace.

The room was dimly lit by candles that flickered off the curtains covering the far side of the room. GJ and the pigeon were whispering behind me, but I couldn't make out what they were saying, as my attention was fixated on the curtains.

"Mother, I'm sorry for taking so long to return with your food, but I met someone who I think you would like to see," Jimi said as he put one hand on the edge of the fabric.

"Jimi, please tell me you didn't disobey my only request. You all promised me you would respect my wishes. Please give them my apologies and show them out," Bissy replied. Her voice was as beautiful as always, even though it sounded incredibly strained and tired.

Before Jimi could defend his decision to break his word, I gathered myself and interrupted. "Forgive him,

Bissy. I am family, though, and the Bissy I knew would never turn away family!" I said with a little chuckle.

"There's no way! Are my frail ears deceiving me? Come here now. I can't get up to run to you. I'm going to cry," Bissy replied, already choking up.

My own tears were already flowing before I could pull back the curtain. As I stepped in, we both broke down, wailing in happiness and sadness from how long it had been.

"How is this even possible? Oh, GW, my dear, you look as if you haven't aged a day since I last saw you. Hug me already. What are you waiting for?" Bissy said, extending her arms towards me.

I didn't hesitate, and fell right into her, embracing her with my entire body and soul. "You know, Bissy, to my body, it has only been a few months, while to you, it has been over twenty years, but you still look more beautiful than I ever will," I joked.

"If you call being on your deathbed beautiful, then I think whatever happened in those sleep machines took all your brain cells," Bissy quipped. It was refreshing to see that even in her frail state she still carried her fiery sense of humor. "GJ?" she called.

"I'm here, Mother. I don't mean to interrupt, but you need to eat and take your pills!" GJ said as he stepped in from behind the curtain with the same confusion in his eyes that he'd had when I came down the stairs.

"You've met your step-nephew, Jimi, but have you met your nephew, GJ?" Bissy asked.

"He looks like a younger Rud, if you ask me. It's a pleasure to meet you, young man," I said, reaching out to shake his hand.

He didn't reach back, and left my hand hanging there. The look on his face was pure anger—or was it distrust? I couldn't quite tell. All I knew was that he was far from impressed that I was here.

"Mother, you need to eat and take your meds. You know what happens when you wait too long. Seeing as Jimi brought back unwanted company, Jacky is out doing a perimeter sweep now, and I must go work the screens, just in case," GJ said, placing a few pills on the nightstand and a plate of food on her lap, then turning tail back out of the room.

"Well, that sure went well. Why are you hiding down here, Bissy? Jimi almost killed me for saying your names in public. What the hell are they watching for? Why was Jacky following me? Better yet, what happened to Rud? I have so many questions."

"I, too, have many questions for you, but I fear that I don't have enough time left to hear your answers or answer all of your questions. I'm already on borrowed time. Pass me that water, and the book beside it, would you please?" Bissy said before grabbing her pills and chucking them into her mouth.

The green leather-bound book was massive. It read *The Watchers* in gold foil letters down its spine. It was heavily used, and as I handed it to Bissy, I saw the author's name: Rud Tailfall.

"Most of the answers you're seeking are within these pages. So, can you humor an old lady and just take tonight to catch up and leave the heavy stuff for tomorrow? After taking these pills, I'll be out like a light in no time," Bissy said, coughing horrendously before putting her hand on mine and offering me the smile that I had dreamt for far too long of seeing again.

We sat there for about an hour, crying and laughing. Most of the laughing was at my expense, but I enjoyed every minute of it. I told Bissy about Nikki, leaving out that she was, in fact, a human until the very end, which gave Bissy plenty of ammunition to tease me with. She enjoyed the part about Nikki disappearing on me mid-kiss almost too much.

As we were laughing, Jacky interrupted us when he returned from his perimeter check to report the all-clear to Bissy. It was bothering the hell out of me as to why they were hiding down here and why there was so much need for secrecy and security, but I had told her I would entertain her tonight instead of asking questions, so I left it alone.

As the night progressed and the laughs continued, I could tell she was fading. I selfishly wanted to keep her up chatting all night, it felt so good to be among family again, but after repeated visits from GJ and Jimi to remind her she needed to rest, I finally sided with them.

Before she'd dozed off, though, she asked me to look after GJ, Jimi, and Jacky when she was gone. She didn't get into the details, but she was persistent in making sure I promised her before finally closing her eyes. Thinking nothing of it, I kissed her on the forehead and closed the curtain behind me.

I went searching for Jacky to ask him a few questions, as GJ had locked himself in one of the other rooms with Jimi. They were obviously discussing me, as when I knocked, I was met with silence.

I found Jacky sitting on the steps in the main entrance, and he gestured for me to sit beside him. "So, you know I have to ask: What were you doing tailing me and my friend? And why did you bolt when we saw each other at the park?" I asked.

"I can't really get into the details yet, but I wasn't there for you. I only followed you because King Gutta Gutta gave you a letter. What was in it? And why did he have you bring it to Augustus?" he answered.

"I wish I knew what was in the letters, but we were doing it to get our friend, who was being held by KGG. It was a job, per se. What about the park?" I replied.

"I didn't know who you were, and thought you may have been there for me. Now that I know that wasn't even remotely true, I feel almost ashamed of running. Try not to bring that up to the other guys, will you? They don't need any more ammo to tease me with," Jacky replied. "You have any ideas as to what was in them letters?"

"You have my word; I never saw you at the park," I said with a wink before continuing about the letters. "If I were to guess, I would think it had to do with the disappearances, or maybe the frog fights. Not sure, to be honest, but I can tell you that Augustus seemed rattled after reading it."

"If it was about the disappearances, it may as well have been about the frogs," he said.

This piqued my interest, and I tried to press him as to what he meant, but he avoided it like the plague and said that only Bissy could answer those questions, so

I gave up on the topic and asked him if there was any way to make a call. I had left Deelow high and dry at the park, and needed to let them know I was okay.

"Nah, man. There's only one phone here, and it can't make regular outbound calls. If you want, I can fly over there and give them a message. I wouldn't mind the fresh air, and I need to do my overwatch night run anyways," he offered.

"If you're going towards the inner city, I would love that. They're probably sitting around getting high and sweating over what happened to me as we speak. Tell them to meet me tomorrow around noon at the basketball courts."

"Not a problem at all, man. Bissy says you're family, so it's the least I can do," he exclaimed before standing up.

I gave him the directions on how to get to Niko's from Founders Fountain. It was the easiest landmark to use, and probably the only one we both knew. We shook hands and he departed—oddly, without letting Jimi and GJ know.

After he left, I headed back to the room where Bissy was sleeping, laid down on the couch just inside the doorway, and fell asleep. I should have taken some time to read some of the book, but the emotional roller coaster of the day knocked me right out almost immediately after lying down.

There was no natural light down here, so I had no idea what time it was when I woke up. There were no candles lit, and the lights were all off, so I thought it was still the middle of the night. There was, however, some flickering light in the hallway that caught my attention, so I cautiously made my way out of the room so as not to wake Bissy.

As I came out past the doorway, I could hear Jimi and GJ whispering to each other, so I quietly knocked on the partially open door. "Just let him in, GJ. You carry part of his name, for fucks' sake. He's family, whether you like it or not," I could hear Jimi say, which was met by a big sigh from GJ.

I had only seen the hallway and Bissy's small room at this point, so as the door rolled back, I was shocked at the size of the room. It was massive. I would say it was almost as large as KGG's warehouse, minus the glossy floors and chandeliers. Each corner had its own curtained-off bed, and there was a kitchen along the back wall. There were shelving units stockpiled with all sorts of food and random boxes on the right wall.

Meanwhile, the two of them were sitting in front of a wall of TVs to the right, each about four times the size of the one in Notorious Meg's office. It looked as if they had cameras situated in every nook and cranny of Gutter City.

"Holy smokes, this is incredible! How many cameras are connected to this? Like, there's Founders Fountain, the Sewer School, Notorious Bar and Grill, the junkyard, and even the trailer park in Dog Town. I can see everywhere I've been on here! You have to have every corner of the city covered," I said, trying to break the ice.

"There are more than I can count, but it gives us a good idea as to what's going on. They also aren't all ours. The ones you see on the left half of the screen are pulled from the Air Patrol, which is kind of like a police force, but super crooked. The ones on the right are our own.

We're missing a few areas, though, like the Rat Kings' territories and the exterior walls, as the frogs take them out fairly quickly," Jimi said, prompting a quick slap to the arm by GJ when he mentioned the frogs.

"I've seen some of the fighters practicing, but I thought the frogs would stay out in the Dead Tree Valley, far from the walls," I said inquisitively.

"You'd think that, wouldn't you? But lately, that has been far from the case. I've seen some even within the city walls—testing the waters, so to speak," Jimi replied. GJ was now glaring at him with angry eyes.

This was as good of a time as any to try to ask all the questions I could. Remembering the KBC tattoo on the fighter at King Gutta Gutta's gym, I swung for it. "I read a lot about the banishment, but there was nothing about what happened after. Has anyone seen King BaCroak's son since?" I asked, hoping I would get some answers, and luckily it looked like I just might.

"He hasn't been seen in years, but I'm pretty sure we have a good idea of where he is and what he looks like," Jimi replied.

"He's with King Gutta Gutta, isn't he?" I asked, swinging for the fences now.

Jimi looked stunned and turned to GJ immediately. They both stayed silent, passing looks between each other as if they were trying to figure out how much to say.

GJ broke the silence. "Why would you say that, and what make you think we know anything about his whereabouts?"

"I did catch Jacky spying on a boxing match at KGG's warehouse, and one of the fighters was tattooed to all hell, and in the middle of his back was a KBC with a crown over it. He spoke to KGG more like an equal than a fighter. Kind of a connect-the-dots kind of guess."

"Interesting. So, you're telling me that you think KGG has let King BaCroak's son back into the city? You think he's working with the Frog King and betraying his fellow rats?" GJ snipped back with a hint of suspicion in his voice.

"Between us, yes, I think he's let him back in, and I think he has some sort of agreement with him, but do I think he's betraying his fellow rats? No. No, I don't."

I didn't like the suspicious tone in his voice or the looks he was giving me; they were really off-putting. This was the most information I had gotten in a long while, though, so I figured I would give him a subtle jab and see if he would confirm my own suspicions. "I think you believe the same, because if you didn't, why would you have had Jacky there snooping around? Isn't that right?"

GJ wasn't impressed, sitting back in his chair, grabbing a pack of cigarettes off the table, and lighting one up. Jimi couldn't help but laugh and affirm my prediction by looking at GJ and saying, "He's got you there."

As he put his cigarette out in the ash tray, a grim look took over GJ's face, and he stood up and started going through each of the cameras. "Shouldn't Jacky have come back from his overwatch run by now? Where was the last place you saw him Jimi?" GJ said, moving quicker through each of the screens.

"I haven't. I honestly thought he was already back," Jimi replied.

"Maybe he's hanging out with my friends. He said he was going to fly by their place to let them know I was okay and to meet me at the park at noon. Maybe he's coming back with them?" I chimed in, causing GJ to reel around angrily.

"Where do they live? Show me now!" GJ shouted, pointing to the wall of screens.

I scanned through, trying to see if I recognized any landmarks close to their place, but the closest I could find was Founders Fountain. I gave them the same directions I had given Jacky, and they found a camera on the same corner Big Lou and I had collided on.

They frantically rewound the footage and saw that he had come through the frame hours ago and went back out of the frame a few moments later. He'd clearly come and gone; he didn't stay.

"This is not good. Not good at all. Check the next few cameras, and let's figure out which way he went. GW, I'm going to need you to ask your friends what the fuck he said, and if he said anything about making any other stops. Also, don't even think about bringing them back here or telling them where you are. I shouldn't even let you go see them, but we may have bigger problems, and I need to know if they have any information," GJ said.

Bissy was still asleep when I went to check on her, so I headed out to meet the boys at the park, leaving the other two to scrounge through the footage as they tried to track Jacky's steps.

My eyes took a while to adjust to the brightness of the day after being underground for almost an entire day. I stopped at the opening on the cliffside, which reminded me of the outlook in the augmented reality that I had shared first with Rud and then with Nikki—albeit, the view was a sprawling city with no creek running through it and no mountains in the distance. Nonetheless, the feel of it was very much the same, and it was beautiful, but with everything going on, I just couldn't enjoy it.

When I arrived, Niko and Deelow were sitting on the bleachers smoking a joint and waiting for me. They were smiling from ear to ear and were eager to hear how it went. "Bro, we can't believe you did it! We were worried to all hell when you went MIA, and glad we were home when your new friend came to give us the news. So, give us the details. You must be on top of the world right now!" Niko exclaimed.

"To be honest, I don't even think I've had enough time to compute it all. Rud, sadly, passed not too long ago, and Bissy is very sick, but being able to see her smile and to catch up was emotional beyond words," I answered, tears starting to well up again just thinking about last night.

Deelow, noticing the tears, wrapped his arm around me and said, "Oh, dude, I can only imagine the emotions you're going through. That story you told about how you were separated was intense, and thinking they were dead this whole time! I still can't believe it, so I can see how you wouldn't have had time to compute it all."

As my tears welled to the point of breaking past my eyelids, I couldn't help but think about how much I'd used to think I was cursed. But after waking up, I had met these two amazing souls and reunited with Bissy and her new family. How could I ever say I was cursed again?

"I can't tell you guys enough about how grateful I am for having met you two. I love you guys! Thank you for everything. You truly have become brothers to me. If I can ever repay you in any way, please do not hesitate to ask!" I said as I hugged them both before wiping my tears and gathering myself.

"Helping get Deelow out was payment enough for me, but you still owe me for that hat! What about you, Deelow?" Niko replied.

"Nah. As I said to you before, GW, your friendship is payment enough for me. Can't have enough good people like you two in my life!" Deelow said.

Unfortunately, they didn't have any information on Jacky, as he hadn't stayed for any more time than necessary. He had asked about the stash of robotic arms and legs that were strewn all over their apartment from Niko's last run outside the walls, but who wouldn't? I know I was incredibly interested, and asked him to save me some pieces to play with when I got back.

They even asked if I wanted to live with them full-time, but wouldn't accept any answer until I had enjoyed some more time with Bissy. I was speechless, and told them again how grateful I was. I promised that I would come back by their place in a few days, and we all hugged again before I went back to check on Bissy and the others.

The walk back went quickly, as I was gushing with happiness. It was almost too much to handle, but I should have taken my time in the moment, because when I returned, so did the curse.

I could hear screams from below as I opened the tree door to the stairs and bolted down the stairwell, through the small hallway, and into Bissy's room. "Mother!? Mother, no!" GJ kept repeating over and over.

I pulled back the curtain to find the two of them slumped over holding Bissy's lifeless body. She was sitting up and smiling, yet her eyes were closed, and there was no sign of breathing.

As I walked over to join the two of them at her bedside, GJ lashed out at me. "Get the hell out of here! This is your fault! First Jacky, and now Mom! *Get out!*" he screamed, tears gushing from his eyes.

"GJ, don't. Did you see the smile Mother had last night when she was with him? And Jacky was on his overwatch, so you can't blame him for that! Neither are his fault. They're no one's fault," Jimi yelled back.

I didn't know what to say, nor did I want to go. I froze in place, causing GJ to lash out again and again. "Get out! Get the fuck out! Why? Why? *Why?*" he yelled.

Before I knew it, my legs started to move, and the next thing I knew, I was reaching out and pulling GJ in. Within seconds, he was hugging me back, crying deeply into my chest. I held him as he soaked my fur with his tears and his yelling slowly turned into murmurs and sobs.

As GJ was still buried into my fur, Jimi bent over, whispering farewells into Bissy's ear. None of us had noticed the pen she held in one hand or the pad in the other until Jimi had leaned in and accidently knocked it out of her hands. He turned to us and, through his tears, began reading its contents out loud.

Boys, I'm sorry that I must leave you like this, but my time has come, I can feel it. I love you dearly, and hope you can forgive me for not being able to hold on any longer.

There's a personal letter for each of you in my nightstand, but with the arrival of my long-lost brother, your uncle, I felt that there was more to be said.

GJ, I imagine this will be the hardest for you to hear, but I hope in time you will understand why I'm about to ask this of all of you.

You're all Watchers now, and with that comes great responsibility and sacrifice. The sacrifice of your own pride is what I ask of you today, as it's my dying wish that GW take my place as the head of the table. I've given him your father's book, and I trust that he will not only look after you all, but that he will also have the strength and heart to do what needs to be done when the time comes. I trust that you all will.

As we all know, the time is near, and our enemies are readying for war. Remember: be kind to each other, love each other, and most of all, protect each other and the ones who can't protect themselves.

Please help GW help you.

I love you all,

Your Mother,

Bissy xoxo

P.S. GW, I'm sorry to disappear so quickly, just as Nikki did to you, but please know that I always loved you, Rud always loved you, and we never forgot you. Remember what you promised, not only last night. You're the last lab rat. The boys need you. The city needs you.

If I could have, I would have broken down right then, but the P.S. got me. If Bissy could find humor in her last moments and have so much trust in me after so many years, then I could be strong enough to keep myself together until I was alone.

GJ and Jimi were in shambles, and Jacky was still missing. Jimi and GJ couldn't wait for him to return to bury her. It was rat tradition to hold the burial on the same day of one's passing, and I wasn't going to take that away from them or her.

After a few hours of uncontrollable tears and angry outbursts, we carried her up the stairs and to the cliff-side where Rud, Tex, and Trix had been buried. It was a beautiful spot just past the main opening that overlooked the city. We all made quick work of preparing the plot and laid Bissy to rest before starting the tributes. It was customary in rat culture for only one main eulogy reader, but I thought it would be best if both Jimi and GJ spoke, and they both agreed.

We had covered her in a white sheet, as I knew I wouldn't have the strength to cover her beautiful smile with dirt. I barely even had enough strength as it was. I was shattering inside, telling myself over and over, *You promised. Hold it together. You fucking promised.*

When tears started to seep out while the dirt thumped off the sheet, my anger started to take over. I began to chastise myself in my head. *She trusted you to be strong. Don't be a bitch. Hold it together.*

After they both finished up and I put the last shovel full down, the three of us sat on the ground, arm in arm, foreheads meeting in the middle, creating a teepee of sadness over top of her grave, collectively creating a pool in the middle of us with our tears.

Suddenly, we heard what sounded like wings beating in the distance, causing us all to race to our feet.

I was expecting to see Jacky racing home, but the sound was off; the wings were not beating in unison. When we finally saw him approaching, I could tell something was terribly wrong. Only one wing was beating fully, and the other was mangled, blood-soaked, and missing almost all its feathers. Half of his face was caved in, and you could even see part of his rib cage on the same side as the mangled wing. It was a horrifying sight as he crash-landed in front of us at the foot of her grave, turning the pool of our tears red.

My medical training from the augmented reality clicked in without a thought, and I found myself barking orders to the other two. "Bandages now! Rip your shirts and give them to me. GJ, tie off his wing and make it as tight as possible. Jimi, I need you to carry him down while I cover and hold his ribs. We need to get him bandaged up ASAP, and by the looks of it, we're going to need to do extensive surgery."

As we were bandaging him up, he was dipping in and out of consciousness. "Guys, I need you to try and keep him talking while I try to stem the bleeding," I shouted.

"Jacky, who did this? Jacky, answer me," they both kept repeating, and to my surprise, he was able to answer, even if it was broken English and half sentences.

"Frogs...outside. Wa...caught....Frogs...coming," he said before passing out from the pain.

GJ and Jimi looked shellshocked and started muttering, "The Frogs are coming. Of all times, they choose now."

Made in the USA
Las Vegas, NV
28 April 2024